SHARON

SHARON

BY

HARRIETT H. CARR

WITH DECORATIONS BY

ARLINE K. THOMSON

HASTINGS HOUSE, PUBLISHERS, NEW YORK

1336640

To my sister Dorothy

ACKNOWLEDGMENTS

To the Director and Staff of Central Branch, Y.W.C.A, and the Director of the Y.W.C.A. Residence, Spelman Hall, in New York City, my grateful appreciation.

CONTENTS

xi

CONTENTS

SHARON

CHAPTER ONE

SCHOLARSHIP TO COLORADO

"EIGHTY-SIX degrees at the Battery at four o'clock," came the radio announcement. For the third straight day New York City was simmering in an unusual May heat wave.

Sharon Heath and Brad Johnson perched in the shade on the top step of a reconditioned old brownstone in the Village. Its new coral-pink façade was much too tropical for a day like this, but the ornamental ironwork in the railing was hard against Sharon's back and gave an illusion of coolness. She pulled her blue jeans above her knees and pressed her slim, bare legs against the rough cement steps.

The house was at one end of the block, and from its entrance she could keep an eye on a little triangular park at the other end where her two younger sisters played. Beside her Brad fumbled with the knobs on his portable radio, searching for some music other than a "tops-in-the-hit-parade" program.

3

SHARON

"What a summer this is going to be!" Sharon groaned. No wonderful vacation for her this year. Daddy was being retired as a professor of chemistry at New York University next month. Instead of taking his family to the cool Maine woods as he usually did, he must teach in summer school and continue the search for a position where retirement at sixty-five was not rigidly enforced. "Senior Citizens" and "Past Sixty Clubs," "geriatrics" and "gerontology" were household words in the Heath family now.

"Maybe the summer won't be so hot. You can't tell," Brad suggested, tuning the radio down to a softer tone. "Anyway, let's go on planning that week on the Cape. Shall I invite Debby Blackwell or not?"

Sharon pushed her short black curls from her forehead. She wasn't sure she wanted Debby included in the group Brad was inviting to his family's summer place on Cape Cod. It wasn't because Debby could go to college in Colorado next year and Sharon couldn't unless she was awarded a scholarship. It was because of Dick Mendendahl, Sharon's cousin, who was graduating in August from the Merchant Marine Academy at Kings Point out on Long Island. The week's visit was to celebrate that important event. Dick was twenty-one years old—five years older than Sharon and Debby—and Sharon thought Debby much too young for him. She was sure to think Dick was her "date," and Sharon was afraid she might act silly. It had happened before.

Brad seemed to know what was on her mind. He knew, too, how she had worried about the scholarship to Colorado. Daddy hadn't thought she would be considered for a financial stipend, since he had his retirement annuity and she could live at home and attend college in New York. That,

4

however, didn't suit Sharon. It would be too much like a continuation of high school. Out in Colorado girls lived together in big dormitories, and the campus practically ended in a ski jump. She could see the folder now, with its colored pictures.

Brad snapped his fingers and waved his hand up and down in front of her eyes.

"There'll be Marie and her boy friend, if she can make up her mind who her boy friend is. There'll be you and Dick and me. Now do we or do we not invite Debby?"

"I'm afraid Dick will be bored with her," Sharon admitted bluntly.

"He probably will be," Brad agreed. "But he'll be sailing the next week for South Africa, or Down Under, or somewhere, so she'll be no problem after that. Besides, he knows she's one of the crowd and he's a good sport. Furthermore, what other extra girl do we know who'll be around?"

"No one I can think of," Sharon said. "All I *can* think of is the end of summer and getting up to your place on the Cape. Cool water, cool breezes and heap big meals."

"Pig! And I'm going to invite Debby."

It sounded final. Sharon looked up at the rather thin and sun-browned face and knew he had made up his mind. Almost eighteen and finishing his first year at New York University, Brad was the leader in her neighborhood group and she respected his judgment.

"I wasn't really objecting," she said. "After all, Debby is my friend and it's your party. She should be along soon. It's time her committee meeting at the Y was over. "She's president of the Y-Teen Planning Committee this year, you know."

5

SHARON

Sharon glanced toward the corner where the street ended at Waverly Place. People were beginning to come home to their Village apartments from jobs all over the city, but Debby was not in sight. Sharon ran one hand over the curlicues and tendrils in the railing and looked down at the greenery in the tiny front lawn. The building would be occupied in another month and she could no longer sit there watching people come and go. Now, however, the superintendent was glad to have her, for she kept her younger brother from throwing his ball against the building, just to prove he could always hit between the windows.

Sharon shook her head at the thought of thirteen-year-old Jimmy. He had been in one scrape after another all spring. She could hear him now, his voice clear and argumentative.

"The Dodgers were not the first organized baseball team!"

"Baseball again," Brad laughed. "How he does not love the Bums!"

"The Cincinnati Red Stockings were the first!" Jimmy's voice sounded positive. He was a Giant fan, so he always said anything he could to belittle the Dodgers.

"I wish he'd grow up," Sharon sighed. For a few minutes they sat quietly watching the group of boys idling in front of the little store across the street where Pop Schmidt sold soft drinks and ice cream, candy and newspapers, and an assortment of knickknacks. He had a television set, and any athletic event on the screen drew a crowd of teen-agers.

"Ebbets Field wasn't their first park either, it was their fourth. Isn't that so, Pop?" Jimmy wasn't going to give in.

"I'll have to go," Sharon said with a sigh. "It's time I broke this up."

6

Brad snapped the radio off and got to his feet slowly. "Are you going to the art show tonight?" he asked.

Sharon nodded. "Marie's expecting both of us. Debby too, so if you don't see her before then. . . ." She left the sentence unfinished.

Brad smiled a big smile. "See you later," he said.

Sharon stopped in front of the store and waited until her brother noticed her. She never tried to tell Jimmy what to do or argued with him when anyone beside the family could hear.

Jimmy's hair was as black as her own and his eyes as deep a blue, but somehow he had acquired freckles like red-haired, nine-year-old Nancy. Sharon and little Cathy, who was eight, had very white skin and they looked alike, Sharon knew. They both had oval faces and noses that tipped up inquiringly.

"Want to help round up the kids?" Sharon called to her brother.

"Time for chow?" Jimmy asked. All meals had been "chow" since the first time Dick Mendendahl had taken Jimmy out to Kings Point. From that day on, Dick had been his hero.

Sharon began walking toward the park. Jimmy would come along if she didn't needle him.

Nancy and Cathy objected to stopping their endless hopscotch game and Jimmy didn't do anything about helping, but the four Heaths finally reached their own three-story home in the middle of a block of small apartment buildings, just as the cuckoo clock in the hall chattered six.

"M-m-m-m-m!" They sniffed approvingly.

7

"Meat loaf! I'll bet it's meat loaf." Jimmy led the procession into the dining room. The drop-leaf black walnut table was open and set with white place mats. A green bowl in the center was rounded with oranges, golden bananas and pears, but Jimmy's eyes turned toward the kitchen.

"I like anything we have for chow so long as it's meat loaf," he announced.

Sharon smiled at her mother, who was carrying dishes of food to the table.

"Go wash up, all of you," Mother ordered. "Scram!" Then she smiled back at Sharon. Her eyes were blue too, and she was slender and her black hair was only slightly touched with gray. Sharon followed her to the kitchen.

"Where's Daddy?" Sharon asked. She wondered if once more he was being interviewed for a job. Appointments and interviews that came to nothing had become all too routine for the head of the Heath family these days.

Mother opened the oven door and filled a dish with baked potatoes. "He should be here now," was all she said. While she was still speaking, the front door opened and Daddy's sure footsteps sounded in the hall.

"Where-you-been? Where-you-been? Where-you-been?" Peeky, the parakeet, shrilled his only recognizable words. Jato, their wire-haired terrier, who had been biting his rubber bone in the back court, began clawing at the screen.

Noise and bluster never bothered Mother. With one free hand she opened the door and the dog raced through the kitchen, a small rocket on legs, to greet Daddy. From upstairs and downstairs bathrooms the scrubbed and shining Heaths converged on the dining room.

Daddy's white hair waved back from his high forehead.

Sharon couldn't remember when it had been otherwise, but Mother said once it had been red. He was a large man with a clear, sandy complexion, and although he was several years older than Mother he didn't look old to Sharon—just dignified, as a professor of chemistry should look.

"All right, everybody," Daddy said when the scramble into chairs subsided. Quieting the noisy Heaths was an accomplishment he managed three times a day. Obediently they bowed heads while he said grace.

"Now what did you all do today?" Daddy asked while he filled the plates.

The separate recitals were interrupted by the clang of the doorbell. Daddy answered it and returned with a letter in his hand.

"It's for you, Sharon," he said and passed it to her. "The mail carrier delivered it at the apartment next door and the super just brought it over."

The envelope was long and white and official-looking, and Sharon knew immediately it was not from any of her friends. This was the letter she had been waiting for. It must be.

She glanced at the return address in the upper left-hand corner and her hopes were confirmed. Her fears, too. The letters in the word "University" were suddenly out of focus and her fingers were thick and clumsy at tearing open the flap.

"My dear Miss Heath:" the salutation began.

"Oh!" Sharon almost gasped and looked at her father. "I'm afraid to read it. I've waited so long, and now. . . ."

"I know how you feel," Daddy sympathized. "I'm almost as excited as you are."

"Hurry up!" Jimmy urged. "Let's get it over. Do you or don't you get to go?"

9

SHARON

" 'My dear Miss Heath,' " Sharon read to herself. " 'We are happy to inform you that you have been accepted for matriculation. . . .' " Her heart was pounding happily, but at the second paragraph it almost stopped.

" 'The University feels a deep sense of obligation, however, to young people of high scholastic standing who cannot continue their education without financial assistance. Our limited scholarships which carry financial aid must of necessity. . . .' "

Sharon knew how the paragraph was going to end without reading it. Daddy had warned her when she applied that it was not likely she would be considered for the coveted scholarship because of his retirement pay.

Sharon had tried to prepare herself for disappointment, but now that it had come, a giant wave seemed to submerge her in a black and treacherous undertow. She read the polite sentences through misty lashes and she couldn't trust her voice. Miserably she handed the letter to her father. Everyone at the table knew what it conveyed.

"Daddy told you," Jimmy said knowingly. Usually Sharon could shrug off his cocksureness, but now it irritated her unreasonably. "It wouldn't be so bad if Debby Blackwell got turned down too," he went on, all too truthfully. "Only she won't. She can afford to pay her tuition."

"Jimmy!" Mother reprimanded. "Debby wasn't applying for a scholarship."

No, she wasn't, Sharon thought bitterly. Debby, who like Sharon loved to ski and swim and did well in all sports, could go to Colorado next year. She'd be able to get away from home and have fun in college. Now, for Sharon at

N.Y.U. it would be more high school in a bigger shop, that was all.

"Sharon'll be all right," she heard her mother saying brightly. "She doesn't have to give up college. She's been accepted by New York University and she'll be all right."

Somehow Mother's brightness was more than Sharon could bear when the thing she had wanted more than anything—ever before in her life—had been denied her.

"Of course I'll be all right!" she stormed. "Only why do things like this have to happen to us? Why does Daddy have to retire? If he didn't, he could send me to Colorado the same as Debby's father is sending her. Where's the justice in my being denied the scholarship? I practically hate these great big inhuman institutions of yours, Daddy!"

She shouldn't have said it. She knew that as soon as the angry words were spoken. Daddy had spent practically all of his life at New York University and she suspected he wanted her to go there.

"Sharon! This isn't like you. Not at all!" There was surprise in Mother's voice, and Sharon felt the blue eyes looking at her reproachfully.

"I'll say it's not," Jimmy agreed. "Whew!" He was staring at Sharon in round-eyed astonishment.

"Yes it is!" Sharon insisted. "It's just how I feel about things that aren't fair. Why should this happen to us, when we can't do anything about it? Why don't bad things happen to bad people?"

"They do, Sharon," Daddy replied handing the letter back to her. "Worse things than being refused a scholarship you don't absolutely need. If you'd been given it, some boy or girl would have been denied a college education. Just so you could have fun skiing. You wouldn't want that on your conscience, would you?"

She put the letter back in its envelope and didn't answer. Daddy pushed his chair back from the table.

"If you'll excuse me, Mother, I think I'll go for the evening paper. Perhaps I'll walk over to Professor Burns's for a minute or two."

Sharon sat staring at her dish, listening to his footsteps while he crossed the living room. Jato tore after him and Peeky shrilled the inevitable "Where-you-been?" Then the screen door clicked shut behind him.

Hurt and defiant still, Sharon got up and began stacking the dishes. She hadn't meant to storm like that. She was surprised at her outburst now that it was over, but to be denied the scholarship . . . to have to tell Brad and Marie and Debby . . . after missing out on her Maine vacation . . . it was almost too much.

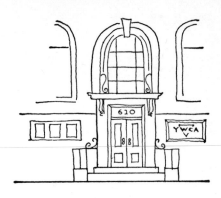

CHAPTER TWO

OUTDOOR ART EXHIBITION

SHARON turned soap powder into the sink and watched the hot water dash it into suds. Across the room Mother was putting food away.

The Heath kitchen wasn't modern and shining and streamlined. The old dark-red brick house had been under rent control ever since that law was passed and the landlord hadn't made an improvement in it for years. The top-floor apartment was occupied by a middle-aged widower who worked in the Public Library and spent all his evenings typing fiercely. He was writing a book and he didn't care how the house looked or whether the owner ever did anything to it. So each time the Heaths suggested repairs they were told the other tenant wasn't complaining.

Mother could understand an author's preoccupation with writing, for she had been a librarian before she married, but she couldn't understand lack of interest in one's home. She

13

had finally painted the kitchen herself. It was a cheerful canary yellow, with a bamboo paper on the wall opposite the sink. Bright birds and an occasional spangled butterfly made it very gay. Sharon liked to work with Mother in the kitchen, but tonight she wished she could be anywhere else.

The rattling of icebox dishes finally ceased and the refrigerator door closed with a brisk bang.

"Are you going over to the outdoor art exhibit with Marie tonight?" Mother asked.

Sharon didn't turn from the sink. "I was going."

"Then I'll keep an eye on Nancy and Cathy," Mother offered.

Sharon rattled the silver, stacked it in the rinsing rack and piled up the plates. "I can do it. I don't have to go," she said reluctantly. Actually she was beginning to wish she could avoid Marie and Brad, and probably Debby too, tonight.

"You run along to Washington Square with Marie," Mother said and at last left Sharon alone.

She needed to be alone. She'd have to think how she would break the news. Laugh it off? Try a "so what" shrug? Pretend she'd expected it all the time? She shook her head at all of those ideas. Her friends knew how much she had wanted to go to college in Colorado. She had never been west of Hoboken except for one trip, years ago, to visit her mother's twin sister in Milwaukee. No, there wasn't any way to hide how she felt, and what-to-say was still unanswered when she had put the last dish away.

Still thinking, Sharon went to her room and changed from blue jeans to a plain rose-colored cotton blouse and a figured skirt in rose and black and white. Marie would want to sketch her again tonight, probably. Hundreds of people milled around the pictures which Village artists brought out from attic studios, basement apartments, and ordinary homes to display on the curb, hang on parking lot fences, or prop against building walls in the Washington Square area. It was the same each time the Washington Square Outdoor Art Exhibit held one of its shows—usually the two weeks before Memorial Day and the first two weeks in September. Occasionally a picture was sold, but more often the spectators moved on with only a word or two about the works which had been so lovingly produced.

Marie's sketching usually drew a crowd, however, and all of her friends were willing to pose for her. She had drawn Sharon so often she could produce a fair likeness very quickly. Besides, Sharon's up-tilted nose was immediately recognizable, and a good portrait influenced visitors to have Marie "do" them.

A last touch of the comb to her softly curling hair, a last check on her fingernails, and Sharon left the house. Only there wasn't much joy in the prospect of an evening at the art show tonight.

It hardly seemed possible that everything on the street could be the same as always—high-pitched laughter from the far end of the block where the little children played, old people filling the benches that lined the cement-paved park, stragglers stopping at Pop's store for a newspaper or a pack of cigarettes before going home. At the end of the block Jimmy was throwing his ball against the reconditioned house while the super was inside eating his dinner. Sharon didn't say anything to him when she walked past. He would be chased away soon enough.

She didn't hurry even when she saw Brad and Marie

15

turning into Waverly Place ahead of her. They looked in her direction and waited when they saw her coming.

"Hurry up," Marie called. "I should be there now."

"Hi, Sharon."

Brad would be philosophical and understanding about the scholarship, Sharon knew, only how she hated to tell him! She looked at her two friends soberly and didn't hurry.

"Come on!" Marie urged and tapped her toe to signal impatience. "It'll be the end of summer before we get there at the speed you're making."

The end of summer! Out on the Cape for Brad and a camp in New Hampshire for Marie. New York for Sharon and nothing to look forward to except the one week with Brad's family and Dick and the rest of the crowd.

Marie Togliotti was a pretty, impulsive girl with lustrous brown hair and the smooth, olive skin of her Italian ancestors. Her features were even and her figure neat and well rounded. She was very attractive and had more boy friends than any other girl in the little group that made up Sharon's world. Her older brother, Frank, and his wife had a copper shop in the Village where they made jewelry and gift specialties at a workbench near the display window of their salesroom. Marie lived with them, helping in the shop after school and on Saturdays. Their parents had remained behind in Italy.

"Marie's afraid that artist who promised to mind her exhibit will sell all of his pictures instead of hers," Brad called.

"Neither of us is likely to sell anything, or win any prizes either," Marie said. "I promised to get back by seven so he could eat, that's all. It's almost seven now."

Sharon quickened her steps and the three hurried to a

16

fence around a vacant lot on the Avenue of the Americas where Marie's sketches hung.

A crazy-quilt splash of color, that's what the blocks near Washington Square looked like to Sharon. Thousands of canvasses, large and small, oils and water colors, crayons and charcoals, all tight-crowded together. Every inch of fence space, every possible building wall, was used to display the works of three hundred or more artists. Marie was exhibiting the best work she had done last year in an evening art class at the Y.W.C.A.'s Ballard School. To her left there were vivid blue and green seascapes painted by an elderly man who worked in a cobbler's shop for a living. A tall, slender Negro boy had the other adjoining space. His half-grown brown and white kitten was riding contentedly on his shoulder, nuzzling now and then against his ear. Everyone who passed stopped to smile at the purring kitten and then look at the paintings.

Brad, who again had his radio, set it on a level spot beside Marie's easel and once more began searching for music he liked. The young artist came over to Marie.

"I didn't sell a thing, but I could have given Scoopy Mewses away half a dozen times," he told her, scratching the kitten's head.

"So you named him for the mythical cat that writes the column in *The Villager?*" Brad said, getting to his feet. "Not bad. He looks like an intelligent kitten."

"And he probably wants his dinner," Marie added. "I'll take over, but don't expect me to be a better salesman than you were."

The Negro boy had been working in water color and most of his pictures were New York street scenes—back-yard jun-

17

gles filled with flapping laundry, fire escapes, flowering window boxes and garbage cans. Sharon didn't particularly fancy the subject matter, but there was rhythm and an arresting use of color in his work. It was much better than the garish seascapes on the other side. He waved at Marie and her friends and started away.

"I'll see you later, and thanks," he said.

"See you," Marie called back and Brad and Sharon waved good-by to him, watching while he disappeared in the crowd.

"Here come some people who look like prospects," Brad said suddenly and turned from the street crowds to look intently at Marie's exhibit. "Come on, kids, get into the act."

"You!" Marie laughed. "Standing there with your head at an angle, trying to look like an art critic."

"Who talked those three gals into sales last night?" Brad asked while Sharon sat down on one of Marie's folding chairs and posed.

The art show had been fun last night. Marie had made five sales. But this was another night and soon other friends would be joining them, particularly Debby Blackwell. Sharon wanted to finish the horrible business of telling about the scholarship before Debby arrived. She didn't have a chance, though, for visitors soon were crowding around to watch Marie work. The first customer was a stout, sweet-faced woman who had to be coaxed by her husband to sit, although Sharon was sure that she wanted a portrait done. Soon the gentleman was telling Brad that they were from Des Moines, that this was their twentieth wedding anniversary, and that he was in the lumber business.

It was fascinating to watch Marie work. She became so absorbed in each new face that she forgot her audience completely. She looked prettier than ever tonight in a simple white smock over a fitted white dress. She was wearing handsome copper bracelets and earrings in a harmonizing design.

"Here come a couple of your admirers," Brad told Marie after she had collected her small fee and said good-by to the tourists. "It's the two who spoke to you in the drugstore last night. And behind them, guess who?"

The girls didn't have to guess. "Is she Miss Village or Miss Park Avenue tonight?" Marie asked.

"I think she's giving us the Park Avenue treatment," Brad replied. "If Debby would just be herself!"

"Maybe she doesn't know who she really is," Sharon suggested. "Maybe if your father had suddenly become a TV celebrity you wouldn't know who you were, either."

Sharon thought that really was the answer to Debby's posing. Debby's father had worked for years as an advertising account executive, then one of his own clients had "discovered" him. Now he was conducting a popular television show and had moved his family to the largest and newest of the elegant apartment houses on lower Fifth Avenue, just off Washington Square.

"I guess she thinks something's expected of her because she's Roy Blackwell's daughter," Marie agreed. "And for that matter, something always is. Working for the Village Fresh Air Fund and this committee and that committee." She shrugged and dismissed the subject.

Debby was a little too thin, a little too tall, and her light-brown hair was unmanageable except for the first day after she had been at the beauty parlor. Today had been the day,

19

Sharon saw when Debby joined them. She was sleek and sophisticated in a black linen suit with turquoise shoes and earrings. The effect was much better than when she tried to be casual and "arty." She arrived just as Marie was introducing two new friends as Hal Newman and Arthur Sutton, his roommate.

"How's the portrait business?" Debby asked as soon as introductions were over.

"Zooming. Breaking all records," Sharon answered for Marie. "New suit, Debby?"

"Comparatively," and Debby gave a self-conscious shrug.

"It looks very, very," Marie complimented her and explained to Hal and Art that Debby's father was a celebrity. They were polite, but it was Marie they had come to see and when she told them they might stop by later and carry her portfolio home, they said good-by and sauntered off.

"Say, where did you meet those two, anyway?" Brad asked Marie as soon as the young men were out of hearing distance. "I meant to ask you last night when they showed up."

"Embarrassing question," Marie replied, frowning.

"You can ignore it, of course," Brad told her. "Only where *did* you meet them?"

Marie took a long breath. "You've got to know, so it may as well be now. I met them when Frank went over to the University with me to see how and where and for how much I could get someone to tutor me in math. Hal's the one."

"Tutor you in math?" Sharon repeated. "Don't tell me you actually. . . ."

"Flunked out, that's what the man said," Marie admitted. "And if I want a high school diploma so I can go on, I have

20

to tutor." She slumped down on her chair and really looked miserable.

"Oh, no!" Sharon sympathized.

"Oh, yes," Marie said glumly. "I could just die. I can't go to art school in Chicago next year unless I work it off, and I'm so afraid I won't get it done before Brad's big party up on the Cape. I've just got no brain for math."

For a moment Sharon stood and stared. Then she almost fell into the other chair. In a way this made it easier to tell of her own misfortune, and she might as well let them all know at once, including Debby who was learning about the party on the Cape before Brad had invited her. Marie must be heartbroken or she would not have been so thoughtless.

"Oh, Marie, you too?" Sharon asked.

"What do you mean, 'me too?'" Marie asked. "You've never flunked anything."

"I mean you aren't the only one with troubles," Sharon told her. "You don't know what disaster is." She stared at her sandals and avoided looking at her friends. "You can go to Chicago all right. You'll work it off. But I can't go to Colorado no matter what I do."

"What?"

"You mean . . . ?"

She could feel them looking at her.

"I can't have a scholarship because we aren't absolutely destitute, and Daddy can't send me because he's forced to retire. So that's that!" Sharon dusted her hands together and then dropped them into her lap, hopelessly.

"And we're both stuck in the city for all summer," Marie groaned.

For a few moments no one had anything to say, then Debby spoke. "You've two new boy friends anyway." She sounded almost envious.

Sharon shook her head. Marie's boy friends were no comfort to her.

"You can always swim at the Y, Sharon," Brad said thoughtfully. "Marie could learn. They've got the announcement of the summer program up already. I saw it yesterday when I was checking on spring hikes they want me to manage. I didn't look at it carefully, but you can be sure of swimming."

"I suppose so," Sharon agreed, but she couldn't be enthusiastic. She and Debby had been swimming at the Y all through high school. That wouldn't be any thrill.

"What about these summer camps the Village Fresh Air Fund supports?" Debby proposed. "Couldn't you go to one of them, or is sixteen too old? All the money we've raised this year with Talent Nights and cocktail parties and style shows and everything."

Debby didn't mean to be patronizing, Sharon was sure, but that was how it sounded and it was more than Sharon could stand.

"Then there's the Sullivan Street Children's Aid Center! I suppose Jimmy and the kids can go there with the rest of the underprivileged!"

"Oh, Sharon!" Debby was contrite. "I didn't mean it that way. I just thought . . . well, we *are* supporting those summer camps. . . ."

She was making things worse all the time.

"As for the Children's Aid Center," Brad broke the awkward silence, "I saw a cute kid there once, about ten years ago. She got her picture in *The Villager*. 'Sharon Heath Elected Miss Pigtails,' the headline said."

Even Sharon had to smile at the recollection of herself winning the prize for the longest pigtails. "Well, let's not talk about it any more," she said. "That's how things are, and that's that!"

"And let's go somewhere else," Brad proposed. "Marie's new bodyguards are coming thisaway. They can do the honors tonight without any help from us. Good night, Marie."

Debby hesitated, but Marie didn't invite her to stay.

"We'll stop at the drugstore opposite your place, Debby, and have a Coke," Brad proposed. "Then I'll walk Sharon home."

"The Brevoort's awfully nice," Debby suggested. "They have a little restaurant."

"Not on my allowance," Brad said. "So long, Marie. We'll be seeing you."

He picked up his radio, clicked the case shut, and they started toward Washington Square, walking slowly in the red and green and purple neon evening. Little French and Italian restaurants, a coffee-expresso place, gift shops and snack bars lined the street, each with tiers of small apartments above the business floors. The people would all be out in the park tonight.

Sharon wondered vaguely if there was another park in the whole world with stationary chess and checkerboard stands where old men played endless games all day and on into the night, until drenching summer rains or freezing winter winds drove them inside. As long as she could remember, old men had matched their skill at those cement game tables while dozens of others stood over them watching every move and muttering now and then. Sometimes competitions were organized, with cash prizes of as much as a hundred dollars for the winner. But prizes or no prizes, the men played continuously. And on the benches that lined the square and criss-crossed it, old ladies sat and stared quietly at romping children, hurrying young people, or the absorbed old men.

"Marie's doing good work," Sharon heard Brad saying. "That sketch of the woman from Des Moines was a *real* likeness."

"I think those she did up at the Ballard School, particularly the ones of the student from Pakistan who was in her class, are her best," Debby commented. "Those and the ones. . . ."

But Sharon didn't hear the end of the sentence. Ahead of them on one of the endless park benches, head bowed in his hands and Jato nuzzled against his knees, was her father.

Never before had Sharon seen Daddy looking old or discouraged. Retirement on an annuity when he wasn't old or incapable of teaching—what did it mean to him? Sharon hadn't thought about how Daddy felt until now. She'd been thinking of herself and how much she wanted to go to college in that fascinating West which she had seen only in colored pictures.

Sharon's jolting step drew the others to a stop and their eyes followed hers.

"You'd better go, Sharon," Brad whispered, but Sharon had already left her friends.

Her father musn't know how close the tears were nor sense the lump in her throat. He must just know she was sorry and ashamed, and hadn't meant to add to his burdens or his unhappiness.

Quietly Sharon slipped onto the bench beside him and

waited. From the center of the park where city bus lines ended came the noise of shifting gears and racing motors. Behind her, a portable radio brought a night game to a small group of baseball enthusiasts sitting on the grass. From every direction came the voices of shouting children, the metallic clang-clang of bicycle bells. But to all the noises and sights and confusion in the park, Daddy was oblivious. At last Sharon reached over and stroked Jato's head and then he turned and saw her. She slipped her hand into his and looked up at him, hoping he'd see, hoping he'd understand.

"My little Rose of Sharon," Daddy said softly and at last he smiled.

CHAPTER THREE

FIRST DAY OF VACATION

THE final weeks of Sharon's last year in high school were busy and they passed quickly. Summer vacation—the first vacation she had spent in the city—started before she could quite realize it had actually begun.

"Sharon, do you suppose you could get lunch today?" Mother asked one Monday morning. "There's an errand I want to do and I'm not sure when I'll get back."

"I guess so," Sharon said reluctantly. "I was going to play tennis with Brad but I guess I could get lunch."

They were clearing away the breakfast dishes and Mother seemed unusually anxious to finish the job.

"Tennis?" she repeated. "I suppose Jimmy could keep an eye on Nancy and Cathy. You aren't going to have many more mornings for tennis with Brad, are you?"

"This is the last."

"Then look, honey. Hurry over to Bleecker Street and get

27

the vegetables from the stands. Things are cheaper there and fresher, too. Don't be afraid to ask prices and look at all of the pushcarts. I've made out a list."

Brad would be there in another hour. Sharon took the list and the grocery money.

"The kids will be all right on the playground if they'll just stay there," she told her mother. "If Jimmy would just see that they stay there."

Mother nodded. "I think Jimmy's ready for more responsibility," she said. "Hurry along so you'll be back when Brad gets here."

Sharon's mind wasn't on the shopping list nor on the lunch she had agreed to prepare. She was thinking of what she would do all summer and what she was going to do about school in the fall. Daddy and Mother were expecting her to go to New York University now. They expected her to decide between being a librarian or a home economics teacher, the careers she had discussed most seriously with them. The very thought of the University had become distasteful to her, however, and the careers she and her friends had more or less accepted seemed rigid and regulated and not appealing at all.

Marie intended to be a commercial artist and Debby talked of a course in dramatic art after she finished college. What was there for girls without a special talent? Sharon wished she had paid more attention to the vocational guidance programs the Y-Teen Club at Central Y had held last year. College in Colorado had been uppermost in her mind then, and it hadn't mattered a great deal whether she decided to take library science or home economics. Now, with the romance of Colorado gone, she wished she were not going to college at all.

What was there to do for girls who didn't go? She decided to find out this summer. There was a guidance counselor at the Y, and although Sharon had never talked to her, she knew of girls who had.

It was quite a walk over to Bleecker Street, where fruit and vegetable vendors lined up their two-wheel carts at the curb and did business from the sidewalk. Green carts and brown carts, crowded tightly together, each with its canvas awning to protect the produce from the sun, each with a small white scale.

Sharon moved from cart to cart with the other shoppers. Most of them were older women and many were speaking Italian. They laughed, or groaned at the prices, and chose each red onion and each zucchini with an appraising eye. From across the sidewalk came the spicy scent of the salamis and cheeses and salads in the delicatessens.

Sharon's bundles were almost as big as she was when she finally started home with her wire tote wagon. Soon she came to the end of her block where the children played, and she knew immediately that something had happened. All of the old people who usually rested on the benches had crowded around one corner of the park. The swings were empty, the games had ceased and the quiet was ominous.

Sharon quickened her steps and strained for a sight of Nancy and Cathy and Jimmy. She couldn't see them, but the crowd suddenly opened to make way for a young man with a child in his arms—Brad, carrying Cathy!

"Brad!"

29

She tried to cry it out but she knew she had barely made a sound. He didn't turn his head. Cathy lay motionless in his arms, her long black curls hanging over his shoulder, her little red play suit a splash of color against his khaki shirt and slacks. Emerging from the crowd behind him came Nancy, white-faced and silent.

"Brad!" His name choked in Sharon's throat.

A bystander saw her and called loudly: "Hey, Brad!" The boy heard then and waited.

Cathy's face was ashen, her eyes closed, and a lump was swelling on her forehead and turning blue. One side of her face was scratched and bleeding.

"What happened?" Sharon gasped. "Oh, Brad, what happened?"

"She fell from one of the swings," he told her. "I'd started to meet you, so I was right here when it happened."

Brad tried to sound calm, but perspiration streamed from his forehead, his voice was thick and unnatural, and his shoulders were bent with the weight of the child. He looked at Cathy's still face, then at the street and the moving traffic.

"Try to get a cab, Sharon," he said. "That one has its signal light on, hasn't it? I'll take her to the emergency service at St. Vincent's Hospital."

Sharon signaled to the driver. "I'll go with you, Brad. I must go," she said.

"You can't, Sharon," he told her while he carried Cathy to the cab. "You can't walk off and leave Nancy and the groceries and everything. And you can't drag all that stuff to the hospital. Open the door for me, please."

She did as he asked and he laid Cathy gently on the back seat.

"There aren't any broken bones, I'm sure, Sharon, honey. Take Nancy home and wait until I call you."

"Somebody's got to be there with her when she comes to," Sharon almost sobbed. "She can't wake up all alone in the hospital."

"I'll be there. I'll send for you if the doctor says you should come. Please go home now and wait until I call."

He took her by the shoulders firmly. "Cathy won't be frightened if she sees me there with her. I'll call you as soon as I know what's what. I promise."

She knew he was right, but she felt faint when the cab pulled away from the curb. Then Nancy began to cry and Sharon had to pull herself together.

"Everything's going to be all right," she said, trying to hide her own uncertainty. "You heard Brad say she didn't have any broken bones. Now stop crying and tell me how it happened."

She wiped Nancy's eyes and gave her a small bundle to carry. "What happened?" she repeated.

"We'd been swinging. Cathy wasn't holding on with her hands. She was holding the ropes in the crook of her elbows."

Sharon could see it all. More than once she had swung like that and almost lost her grip. If only she had been on the playground with the kids. . . .

"Where was Jimmy?" she asked. "Where is he now?"

"I don't know. I should have said something to her, Sharon. I'm older than she is and. . . ."

Nancy's tears were spilling again.

"Now don't cry. Here we are. Open the door for me."

The small front hall was always dismal, and today it seemed positively funereal. Sharon and Nancy deposited

31

their bundles in the kitchen and returned at once to the living room to wait near the phone for Brad's call. They hadn't long to wait.

"Everything's going to be all right. She came to while I was carrying her into the hospital." Brad sounded reasonably confident.

"Is she badly hurt? Was she awfully frightened?"

"She wasn't too frightened. The doctor's examining her now so I slipped out to call you. If I can't bring her home I'll call you again. Okay?"

"Then you don't know . . . Brad, if you can't bring her home I've got to go to the hospital. I must see her."

"Okay, Sharon. If I can't bring her home I'll call you back."

Sharon and Nancy slumped on the davenport and for a time sat hand in hand, staring blankly at the flowered slip covers on the chairs, the dark bookcases that lined one wall, the television set in the corner, now silent and lifeless. It was awful, this not knowing how badly Cathy was hurt.

"Maybe we'd better start making lunch," Sharon said at last. "Do you want to help me or play with Jato in the patio?"

Nancy chose to help Sharon, but she spent most of her time running to the front window to see whether the sounds she heard might be a cab bringing Cathy home.

The wait seemed endless. Sharon set the table, made a salad for lunch, got out the bread for sandwiches. Still Brad did not return. Neither did Jimmy, and Sharon wondered whether Mother and Daddy had any idea of where he might have gone. She had supposed he was watching the little girls. Where could he have gone?

Nancy's shout finally brought Sharon running to the front

door and down the steps. Brad helped a bandaged Cathy out of the car and paid the driver.

"Want me to carry you, Cathy?"

He smiled down at the little girl who stood close beside him looking surprised and bewildered. Then he glanced at Sharon and the light in his eyes told her everything was all right.

"She's fine, but I think she wants me to carry her," he said and took Cathy in his arms again. "The doctor said she is to be kept quiet the rest of today. That's all. She can have all the ice cream she wants."

They were propping her up on the davenport when Mother came home, and before the story had been fully told Daddy arrived, bringing Jimmy with him. Then the inquiring eyes of all the Heaths, and Brad too, turned upon Jimmy.

"How was I to know she'd do such a fool thing?" Jimmy looked from one to another for support.

"Where did you go, instead of staying with your sisters?" Daddy asked. "Where were you coming from when you met me on Waverly?"

"I went over to P.S. 41 where they have a real playground and equipment and stuff," Jimmy explained. "The playground's going to be open all summer, only just for little kids. They told me thirteen's too old, but I could stay this morning. Just this once."

Jimmy was a picture of misery, and Mother relented.

"We won't say anything more about your having left the children alone, Jimmy," she said. "Seeing your little sister like this should be punishment enough. Now let's have lunch. You can stay, can't you, Brad?"

Brad accepted gladly but said he'd call home first. Maybe

33

he and Sharon could still get in one set of tennis before he had to help with the final packing.

"I've got some exciting news for us," Mother confided while Brad was telephoning. "I was talking to the man upstairs last night and he told me the Public Library needed substitute workers during vacations. So this morning I went to see about it. I can work in the libraries all summer, starting here in the branch in the Village."

"Mother! You?" Sharon hadn't thought of such a thing as her mother working.

"Why not? Once a librarian, always a librarian."

"You've surprised us all right!" Daddy stepped back, his head tilted thoughtfully, and Sharon and Jimmy reappraised Mother, too. Blue eyes shining, an alert and eager expression, a neat figure in a tan summer suit and green shoes—yes, she looked like a librarian already.

"What gives?" Brad asked, coming from the hall into the dining room.

"Mom." Sharon answered. "You tell him."

Mother walked to Daddy's side when she told again what she had done, and Daddy hugged her shoulders affectionately.

"Maybe you can get started on your book at last," she concluded. "Summer school won't be so confining, will it?"

Daddy shook his head. "This is going to be a family of breadwinners," he said cheerfully. "Professor Burns tells me I should offer to do tutoring."

"Maybe I can get some baby-sitting to do," Sharon chimed in, but even as she spoke the memory of the morning's near-tragedy came back to her. If Daddy and Mother were both working, how could she do any baby-sitting?"

It was a sobering question and one Sharon didn't voice

until she and Brad were alone that afternoon on their way to the tennis court.

"Your mother's pretty swell, isn't she?" Brad asked. "I don't think my mother could come up with anything like that, if Dad had to retire. You never know, though. Sometimes your folks surprise you." 1336640

"She surprised me all right," Sharon agreed. "And it's wonderful, of course. Only how am I to do any kind of work to earn money if they're both going to be away? And probably crazy hours. The library's open until nine almost every evening and if Daddy does tutoring he'll be on call, won't he?"

"I was thinking the same thing, only I didn't want to say it," Brad admitted. "I sure don't know about trusting Jimmy with the little kids."

"I'm afraid I do!" Sharon said. "I'm afraid I know who's going to do the baby-sitting and where. And for nothing, too!"

They walked in thoughtful silence for several minutes. When Brad spoke he sounded serious.

"I've been thinking about this summer. For you, I mean," he began. "I know you weren't too impressed with my suggestion last night, but it's still the best one I've been able to come up with."

"What do you mean?"

"The Y. They've got a corking summer program lined up. Asked me to take charge of one of the courses at the Craft Studio, and I'd have done it if Dad hadn't needed me to sort of take charge at the Cape part of this summer when he can't be there. You ought to go up to Central and see what they have. You can't just loaf, and baby-sit with Cathy and Nancy."

SHARON

It certainly wasn't what Sharon wanted to do.

"You know how it is at the Y in the winter," Brad went on. "A dozen different things every hour in the day and until ten or eleven at night. Probably the summer schedule is something like it."

"I'll go," Sharon said. "Tomorrow morning if I can get away. I didn't mean to be nasty last night, and I guess I should have apologized to Debby. We've both been swimming at the Y for years, and she's a better swimmer than I am. Maybe subconsciously I'm jealous or something."

Brad smiled a wry smile and shook his head. "I know," he told her. "She was tactless last night. Well, here we are. One set is all we'll have time for. We can go to the movie tonight, though, can't we? There's a swell opera at the Waverly. Some new Italian stars, and Marie says they're something! It'll be our last movie for a while, I'm afraid."

It would be their last movie for two long months. Sharon pushed that horrible thought back beyond the horizon of her mind deliberately and said yes. Brad loved the operas and she enjoyed serious music, although in a more passive way than he. There wasn't any question about their date, however. Mother always let her go to the movies with Brad when there wasn't any school the next day.

They stood beside the tennis court as long as they dared after their play. Three times Brad said he must go, but each time he thought of something more to say.

"If you don't go pretty soon you won't be back in time for the show," Sharon finally told him. "It's hard to follow these Italian operas if we get in late and don't know the score."

At last he left and Sharon started home slowly. Tomorrow morning would start a new life for her; a serious life of learning about careers, getting summer schedules at the Y and finding out what was expected of her at home with both parents working.

She turned from Waverly Place in time to hear Jimmy extolling his Giants once more.

"Whoever did what 'King Carl' Hubbell did in the second major league All Star game?"

"Ready for responsibility!" Sharon said to herself. Jimmy's hands were stuffed in his pockets, and he faced half a dozen neighborhood boys in a defiant pose.

"You know what he did, don't you, Pop?"

Sharon stopped and looked at Pop thoughtfully. His face was ruddy and deeply lined, and his eyes were slits between puffed eyelids.

"Listen!" Jimmy insisted. "There were two American Leaguers on base in the first inning and Hubbell struck out Babe Ruth and Lou. . . ."

Sharon didn't listen to the rest of it. A fine chance she had of doing anything this summer.

"I'm right, aren't I, Pop?"

"Yeah, you're right. Only where do you get all that old-time stuff?"

Pop looked up and spied Sharon. "Where?" he repeated.

"In the sports magazines, I guess," Sharon suggested.

"Only it ain't been in the sports magazines. Not lately at least. I get every magazine there is for my stand here. He's always comin' up with somethin'."

Sharon didn't know where Jimmy "got it," and her mind wasn't on baseball. She would wear her prettiest blouse and skirt tonight—an aqua blouse that was cut away on the shoulders and an aqua and gray skirt. She had new pink slippers to go with the outfit, and pink beads. Brad hadn't seen it yet, and this would be their last date for ages.

After dinner that evening she dressed carefully, and she had a satisfied feeling when she went downstairs to meet Brad. His slow smile confirmed her judgment of the dress and how she looked in it. This last evening together should be a festive one. She wasn't going to say one word about the morning's accident or the sorry summer that stretched ahead, not even when they said good-by.

Brad had brought a picture book for Cathy, and they spent a little time with her before starting for the movie. She was still shaky, but it was apparent her injuries were not serious.

"You two look sharp," Cathy told them when Sharon bent over to kiss her good night. "I think you're my two most favorite people. And I think Brad is better looking than any movie star. Better looking even than Dick."

"Now there's the kind of girl a fellow likes to know," Brad joked. "One who appreciates him."

Sharon wanted to tell him she appreciated him, too. Mother and Daddy had already thanked him for his help with Cathy, and he did indeed look handsome tonight. He had dressed for this last date, too. Probably he was going to take her somewhere special after the show. She would thank him for herself then.

They started down the street hand in hand. Ahead, Jimmy was bouncing his ball on the sidewalk, walking toward Pop's place where some of the boys had gathered to watch a night game on the television set.

"Sharon, where is Jimmy going to play this summer if the school playground is restricted to younger kids?" Brad asked thoughtfully. It was another worry Sharon had been trying not to think about.

"There must be some place. Maybe Daddy'll know."

"If there isn't anything in *The Villager,* call the Recreation Department," Brad suggested.

They both watched the slender figure ahead of them, thumping his ball on the sidewalk and catching it deftly each time. Then, with a sudden twist of his body he let the ball fly against the new pink façade. He threw from an angle, and before she heard the shattering of glass Sharon knew that this time he was going to miss.

"Brad! Oh, no!"

"Oh, yes!" Brad groaned too. "That kid!"

Sharon started toward her brother, but Brad held her back.

"Wait a minute, Sharon. Let's see what he does when the super comes."

The super was there that instant. "You! I warn you a-plenty. Now I go see your old man! He pay for this!"

The man spoke broken English, but his meaning was perfectly clear.

Sharon hurried ahead and met the two while the super was shaking his finger before Jimmy's frightened face.

"You! You trouble maker! You smarting pants! I see your old man now."

"Look, Jimmy can pay for that window himself," Sharon interrupted.

"Him? Pay?"

"Yes, him!" Sharon insisted. "Jimmy Heath, you go right home and get your piggy bank. Get it quietly, too. We aren't going to tell Daddy about this until you've paid for it and with your own money. What a way for you to start the summer!"

Jimmy didn't argue. "Have I got enough? Do you think I've got enough?"

Sharon felt almost sorry for him. His voice was squeaky with fright.

"How much will it cost?" Sharon asked the man.

"Five bucks. He ain't got no five bucks, has he?"

"He should have more than that. If he hasn't, I've got my allowance. Just don't go to Daddy right now."

She turned to Jimmy, who hadn't made a move. "Jimmy! You heard me. Now you go!"

He left on the run, and the super looked at Brad and Sharon uncertainly.

"Has he got it?" Brad asked.

"If he hasn't been shaking it out to spend on popsicles."

Brad turned to the super. "Will it really cost the kid that much?"

"If it cost less I give it back to him," the man promised. Then, "No, I give it to his sister. You his sister, ain't you? You gonna have trouble with that keed."

"I've got trouble!"

Sharon hadn't meant to say it, but this latest mishap pointed things up all too clearly. How was she going to take part in the summer program at the Y, how was she going to earn any money baby-sitting, how was she going to do anything this summer except try to keep Jimmy and Nancy and Cathy out of one difficulty after another? How could she even think about any plan for herself?

Jimmy came back at last and counted out his quarters and

nickles and dimes for the super. Although there wasn't much left in his piggy bank, Sharon did not relent.

"I'll take the piggy bank too," she announced.

A chastened Jimmy did not argue. He stood bouncing his ball against the sidewalk, uncertain what to do next.

"What are you going to do with the pig?" Brad asked when they were out of Jimmy's hearing range.

"Leave it with Pop," Sharon said. "I don't know how Jimmy got it out of the house without being seen. It's too much to expect him to get it back unnoticed. I'll decide how to tell the folks tomorrow."

Pop, who had seen the entire mishap, nodded understandingly when Sharon asked him to keep the pottery pig.

"What that kid needs is a job," he observed. "Something to do. They won't let kids work any more and then blame 'em for gettin' into mischief. Whatta they think?"

Sharon didn't know what they thought. She only knew her last evening with Brad was shattered, and she looked at him ruefully.

"Well, honey, let's pick up the pieces and go on from here," he said and took her hand. "What's a broken window among friends?"

She tried to tell him after the movie when they sat side by side at one of the old-fashioned ice cream-parlor tables in the coffee-expresso house. He had taken off his glasses and was leaning back against the wall, twirling them idly and smiling at her. Around them people were talking about the opera, the play they had seen, an art exhibit somewhere, books they had read or were writing. This was a Village crowd, drinking the rich Italian coffee leisurely, talking leisurely. Sharon

41

stirred the hot whipped milk and cinnamon into her brew and looked at the paintings on the walls, the pieces of sculpture and the people, her mind on the day's events.

"Brad, you know you've been special today, don't you?" she began. "What I mean is, Cathy isn't the only one who appreciates you."

"I like to hear you say it," he said softly and touched his cheek against hers for a moment. "But you know something? I don't feel half as sorry for you tonight as I did the night you told me about the scholarship."

"Why not? This has been one awful day!"

"But you met it, blow for blow!" Brad held her hand up. "The winnah!" His eyes were smiling, and he looked as though he really was proud of her. "The way you handled Jimmy tonight. It's going to be a difficult summer, but you'll make it."

His confidence in her gave her a good feeling. The coffee was comforting and the Village, after all, was home. With the beauty of the opera music still living in her heart, Sharon thought she'd get through the summer too, even though it looked like a long, long time and Brad was going to be far away.

CHAPTER FOUR

A NEW ROUTINE

THE new routine for the Heaths started the next morning with Mother hurrying through breakfast to leave for a special orientation session in library work and Daddy announcing he'd keep an eye on the girls, since he had no classes that morning.

"Then maybe I can go up to the Y," Sharon said hopefully. "Do you suppose I could? This morning, I mean?"

"Do they have swimming in the morning?" Daddy asked while he helped Sharon clear away the dishes.

"I don't know. Besides, it wasn't swimming I had in mind. I want to find out about the summer program and talk to the guidance counselor."

"The guidance counselor?" Daddy set the dishes on the drainboard, and she knew he was watching her. "Are you in the market for some guidance?"

"Don't make fun of me," Sharon said reproachfully. "The guidance counselor knows all about vocations and careers and jobs and requirements, I think. All I know is what I don't want to do!"

"And what don't you want to do?"

Sharon hesitated. "I know you like being a teacher, Daddy, but I don't like being cooped up. I wish there were something I could sort of do myself. Something not so . . . prescribed, I guess."

She turned away as she spoke the words. In spite of her failure to get the scholarship, she was sure Daddy was not going to change his view of her future. Because he had lived all his life in a college environment he had brought his family up to expect a university education to follow high school graduation as surely as lunch followed breakfast and dinner followed lunch.

Sharon scraped and rattled the dishes noisily, and Daddy turned from the kitchen busyness to watch Jato bouncing about in the little back patio, endangering the flowering plants in their pots and boxes with his rubber bone. For a few minutes Daddy was silent, then he walked over to the sink and found a dish towel.

"You know, Sharon, perhaps parents ought to tell their children more about what they're planning and how they expect to carry out those plans," he began while he wiped and re-wiped a cup. "I'm afraid you're taking this matter of losing the scholarship and my retirement too seriously. Are you thinking you should give up your college education? That you can't be a librarian or a home economics teacher as you've always planned? If that's what's on your mind. . . ."

Sharon shook her head vigorously.

"I don't want to any more," she protested. "Daddy, I . . . I wish I didn't even have to see a university. There are things

44

men do. Brad's father has made a lot of money in the real estate business, and Frank's doing all right with his copper craft shop. There must be things girls can do where they'd be on their own!"

"I'm sure there are," Daddy agreed. "It's a good idea for you to see the guidance counselor and find out everything you can. Only whatever you do—have a business of your own, I suppose you're thinking—there's a whole world of ideas and facts and knowledge. A realm of the mind. You wouldn't be happy or satisfied if you shut the door and missed that adventure, because you have a good mind, Sharon."

"I'd still have it. And the university doesn't own knowledge!"

She knew she wasn't being reasonable, and she was glad Daddy ignored her retort.

"What I was getting around to saying is that Mother and I have been planning for a long time. We haven't just sat and waited for the tide to sweep away our house of sand, so to speak. We have educational insurance for Jimmy and Nancy and Cathy, and a nest egg to get you started. I thought maybe you and I could take some time this summer to find out about other possible scholarships or funds, and maybe some college not so far away where you might go for a year at least. We'd certainly want you home for Christmas, and transportation is part of the cost."

Sharon kept her eyes on her dishwashing. She knew transportation was a factor. They'd talked about that before.

"I don't think we really explored all the possibilities," Daddy went on. "You and Debby had your hearts set on that one college."

Once more Sharon listened in silence.

45

"Well, you go on up to the Y and talk to everyone who advises girls," Daddy said at last. "Find out about the swimming schedule too. You're a good swimmer, and there's not much going on around the Village in the summer. What's your financial situation, by the way? Did you have to help Jimmy pay for that broken window?"

Sharon dropped the plates back into the water and stared at him. His eyes were smiling, and his damp hair, waving back from his forehead, glistened where the sunlight from the open door fell upon it.

"Did he tell you?" she asked.

"I was in the court, but I could have heard the super shouting if I'd been up at Times Square," Daddy laughed. "I knew what had happened, all right. Besides, Jimmy was moping around in the rumpus room all last evening. I always know something's wrong when Jimmy goes into seclusion down there."

Sharon knew too. The rumpus room was Jimmy's haven from all storms.

"Jimmy had more than enough in his piggy bank to pay for it, and I've got half of my July allowance left," Sharon said. "I'll be all right. Only I wish I could get some baby-sitting to do. I wish we could depend on Jimmy to watch the kids once in a while."

"I think we can," Daddy assured her. "You run along to the Y."

Sharon was glad she could go. The same old bus ride, the crowded streets, then the big, solid Central Y.W.C.A. building—there was something reassuring about the spacious lobby, the familiar face of the older woman behind the information desk. Above her a large red and blue sign an-

46

nounced the summer program. "Recreation—Education" it said, and perched on the big letters were lively drawings of girls diving into the pool, dancing on the roof, and sitting at typewriters.

It was the girls at typewriters that caught Sharon's eye. She had thought more than once of learning to type. Several girls in high school typed their school themes. Daddy had an old typewriter in the little room that he called his den. That was where he intended to write his book some day.

The bulletin rack beside the elevator was filled with leaf-lets as always. Green and white posters explained the summer activities at Quannacut Camps for younger girls; bright red and blue ones identified the Teen Club which Sharon had joined during her last year in high school, and a new sheaf on salmon-colored paper listed summer activities.

"Learn typing this summer at Ballard School, Central Branch," Sharon read, and there was the schedule and list of fees. She had always thought of the Ballard School as a pro-gram for adults, and mainly an evening-school program. Ma-rie had said most of the people in her art class were older than she and had talked of classes in upholstery and cooking and metal crafts. But the new salmon-colored leaflet said plainly "For High School Age Students."

It was just like everything else at the Y—organized so you couldn't miss. Gay and colorful and perky. The illus-trations showed boys and girls sitting at typewriters that fairly smiled. You could almost hear the keys singing.

MASTER THE KEYBOARD
GAIN SPEED AND ACCURACY
LEARN BUSINESS FORMS

Sharon read every word with a growing conviction this was for her. What was left of her July allowance wouldn't pay for the full course, but maybe she didn't have to pay it all now. Graduation expenses had been so much more than she had anticipated that she'd had to ask Daddy for an advance, and she didn't want to do that again.

She began re-reading the announcement. By the end of summer she should have mastered the keyboard, gained speed and accuracy and learned about business forms. What could that mean? A job, maybe?

What about typists' jobs? She would ask the guidance counselor. It probably meant regular hours, the same as teaching, but hadn't she heard that typing often led to something else, and if she could earn money next year—until she made up her mind what to do—after all, she was a year younger than most high school graduates. But how would Daddy and Mother react to such a program?

Sharon's pondering was interrupted by a familiar greeting. "Hi, Sharon! Going swimming?"

It was Debby Blackwell, who had come in with two other girls while she was studying the announcements. They were waiting for the elevator.

Sharon shook her head. "Not today, I guess."

"Oh, come on! Who do you suppose is instructor this summer?"

"Who?"

"Sally Moore! She's got a swell bunch signed up for the morning class. Come on."

Sharon hesitated. Miss Moore had been an assistant swimming instructor last year, and Sharon thought she was wonderful. Twenty years old, pretty, an excellent swimmer and

48

teacher, Miss Moore had been a favorite with all the girls.

"You don't have to sign up for the whole course unless you want to," Sharon heard Debby saying. "You can just pay the pool fee for today. That's all I'm doing, for I won't be here after this week."

Sharon felt her cheeks grow warm. Must Debby remind her of the difference in their summer plans, too?

"Come on," Debby urged. "Here's the elevator. You're an awfully good swimmer and Miss Moore'll be glad to see you."

Sharon had never been particularly clothes-conscious, but standing in the elevator with Debby in her expensive summer cotton, Sharon wished she had put on something beside the same old rose-colored blouse and skirt she had been wearing all spring. She hadn't expected to see Debby and hadn't thought about her clothes, except to be sure they were clean and pressed. Once they were in the uniform bathing suits the Y provided, however, clothes wouldn't matter.

The sight of the pool, the green of the water and faint smell of chlorine, were a delight to Sharon, and there was Miss Moore in her red bathing suit, her heavy chestnut hair curling tightly all over her head, brown eyes shining with welcome.

"Sharon Heath! I didn't dream of seeing you!"

Miss Moore held out a hand, then gave Sharon a quick hug. She turned to the girls who were clustering about at the entrance to the pool.

"What about your medical exams, girls?" she asked. "You have to be checked up every six months in order to use the pool or gym, you know. Anybody who hasn't been?"

There were two newcomers without medical records,

and Debby volunteered to take them to the medical office.

"I don't suppose you're going to sign up for the course either," Miss Moore said, watching Debby and the girls leave. "It would be wonderful if you were with us for the full season."

"I don't know," Sharon hesitated. "Debby won't be here this summer, but I will."

"You will? Oh, then you must come. With you in the group we could do things. Maybe really put on something."

Miss Moore wasn't questioning why Sharon would be in the city. She was *glad* about it, and she wanted Sharon in her group. What a relief, not having to explain. Sharon found herself wanting to sign up for the course.

And she loved to swim. There wasn't a stroke she hadn't mastered. Debby could outdistance her and Debby almost never missed on a dive, but her form wasn't any better than Sharon's.

Sharon hurried to the lockers and into the bathing suit she had checked out, then jumped into the pool. She kicked deep from her hips and her hand cupped the water just right. This was fun, and Daddy had said she should find out about swimming schedules. She laughed with the others, and the room resounded with shouts and splashes and happy hoopla.

Miss Moore blew her whistle for attention.

"Come on, girls! I want to see what you really can do. This is a very good group. You're real swimmers, most of you, and the beginners will improve. Now cross the pool with the breast stroke."

The instructor's enthusiasm was contagious and her smile made everyone happy. The girls lined up at the starting

point and went through the crawl and over-arm, anxious to do
their best for her. Her eyes moved quickly from girl to girl,
shining with encouragement, measuring each one's skill.
Sharon stopped to talk with her after the session was over.

"I'm finishing up at Columbia this summer, and was I glad
to get this job," Miss Moore told her. "I hope we can make a
real showing. Something more than just keeping the pool
open and doing guard duty. You'll be back, won't you? There
are some good swimmers here, all about the same size, and
if I had you. . . ."

Miss Moore looked down into the pool, where the water
was quiet now. She had something on her mind.

"I'd like to," Sharon admitted. "I'll see what Daddy says.
I'd about decided to take the typing course and I do have to
help with the kids at home."

"Tell him you'd be the key person in this group," Miss
Moore said and again gave Sharon's shoulders a hug. "The
very *key*, if I can go on with what I have in mind."

"What is it? Or shouldn't I ask?"

Miss Moore thought a moment, then lowered her voice.
"They've never had anything except routine in the summer
here at Central," she said. "No water ballet or Aquacade or
anything like that. Usually the summer groups come and go,
but these girls are surprising and they're going to be here all
summer. It would be a grand break for me if I could make a
real showing. But I'd need you, or someone like you. Someone who can really swim and who's had experience."

Sharon thought she understood. This was the first time
Miss Moore had been in full charge. Of course she was eager
to do an outstanding job. Sharon wondered what she was going to do after she finished at Columbia, but this wasn't the

time to ask. They were walking toward the showers and lockers.

"Anyway, come as often as you can," Miss Moore said as she left Sharon.

Sharon thought of the Aquacade last spring while she took her shower and dressed. It had been the big "spectacular" every spring for years, and she had taken part twice. She and Debby had been the two to hold the center spoke positions last spring. Miss Moore had helped but hadn't been the one in charge. What an event that had been, with a large crowd to watch, refreshments afterwards, and dancing on the roof. Dancing with Brad!

Debby and the girls she came with had gone when Sharon left the dressing room. She had mislaid her announcement of the Ballard School program, so she took another from the rack when she left the building. The best thing to do was to tell Daddy about the whole program and see what he thought. He was the one she would have to work out time schedules with, now that Mother wasn't going to be home all day as in the past.

Sharon didn't think of the girls' counselor until she was on the crosstown bus going home. It scarcely seemed she needed to talk to the counselor, though. She thought she knew what she wanted to do. If only she could get the time. If only Jimmy were more dependable.

Sharon began looking for Jimmy as soon as she turned the corner from Waverly, and she saw him almost at once. He was lying on the top of a shining new automobile near Pop's store, arms and legs dangling over the sides of the car. He'll be the next one to fall and get hurt, Sharon thought to herself. How was she to get him to come down, and where were Nancy and Cathy and Daddy?

Sharon didn't have to get him down. A sliding screen was jerked from an open window in the apartment above him and a woman's head popped out. It was a carefully waved, blonde head and the woman appeared to be stout, middle-aged, and angry.

"Young man, you get off that car and stay off! Our new car!"

Jimmy obeyed at once. He clambered to his knees, crawled to the back of the auto top, slid down to the engine hood of the car next to it and in less than a minute was on top of the adjoining car.

Sharon glanced at the woman, who was putting the screen back in the window.

"Just stay off our car, that's all," she scolded.

Sharon stopped in front of Jimmy's latest perch. "Where're the kids?"

"Up at the playground. Dad's with them. I stayed for hours and hours. I thought you'd never come home."

It didn't sound much as though Jimmy was going to like the summer assignment she had in mind for him.

"When they chase you off this car, you'd better come up to the park," she suggested. She didn't really want him there just now.

Daddy saw her coming and moved over on the bench to make a place for her. "How'd it go?" he asked.

Sharon told him everything and gave him the announcement. He read it thoughtfully and nodded.

"Typing is a good skill to have," he said. "Whatever you

53

do. And you should sign up for swimming, especially if you can help Miss Moore on her first job. Here comes Mother. We'll see what she thinks."

Sharon had expected Daddy to question her more. She wondered if she should tell him what she really had in mind. Would he agree that she should take typing if he knew she was thinking about a job next September?

She didn't have time to decide whether she should say more. Mother, with a letter in her hand, stopped in front of them. She didn't look pleased.

"It's from my sister Agnes in Milwaukee," she began. "We're going to have a house guest for the next few weeks."

"A house guest?" Sharon asked, moving over to make room for Mother on the bench.

Mother handed the letter to Daddy.

"Your cousin Janice Ross," Mother explained. "You remember the time we spent Christmas in Milwaukee with Aunt Agnes, don't you? I guess Janice will have to share your room."

"Share my room?" Sharon repeated. "It's too small, especially these hot nights. Why does she have to stay with us?"

Sharon couldn't remember much about her cousin Janice, but the prospect of two girls in that small bedroom was most unpleasant.

"Your Aunt Agnes says she shouldn't be alone just now. They're going to pay for the room. Agnes insists and I guess we'll let her do it. Sharon can have the money, can't she Daddy?"

The prospect of the money was welcome.

"How old is she?" Sharon asked.

"She's nineteen," Mother replied and sighed when she

said it. Daddy gave the letter back to her and didn't say anything.

"How much am I going to get?" Sharon asked. She hoped it would be enough to pay for both swimming and typing. There probably would be expenses for books and paper too.

Mother and Daddy were both staring at the broken pavement at their feet and neither answered her.

"How much?" Sharon asked again.

"What? What did you say, Sharon?" Mother asked and the small lines in her forehead deepened into a worried frown.

Sharon got up and looked at them. They weren't paying any attention to her, and they both looked serious.

What was wrong with this Janice Ross and her visit to New York? Sharon wondered. Something, that was certain. Was Janice going to interfere with her plans now that she had found something she could do, and wanted to do?

CHAPTER FIVE

NEW YORK MEANS GLAMOUR

SHARON'S curiosity about her cousin mounted in the next few days. Daddy and Mother avoided talking about Janice, and Daddy's answers to Sharon's questions were non-committal. She decided to meet Mother when the branch library closed Friday night and walk home with her. Mother often talked to Sharon as though she were grown up when they were alone. Those were the times Sharon liked best. She asked about Janice as soon as they were out on the street.

"You should remember Janice," Mother answered. "We spent one Christmas in Milwaukee, remember? She was a nice little girl."

Sharon's recollection of that holiday and the Wisconsin relatives was very vague. She scarcely remembered Janice at all.

"She isn't peculiar or sick or anything, is she?" Sharon pressed.

"Of course not," Mother answered. "What makes you think anything is wrong with her?"

"You didn't sound very glad to have her come when you got that letter," Sharon reminded her mother.

"Well, I have my hands rather full," Mother admitted. "And if you're going to enroll for two courses at the Y, you aren't going to be much company for her. Then she's two years older than you. To tell the truth, Sharon, I don't know what we're going to find for her to do for all those weeks.

"Maybe she likes to swim," Sharon suggested.

"I hope so. But if she's anything like your Aunt Agnes. . . ." Mother shook her head and looked at the dingy stores and apartment buildings they were passing. Fire escapes dangled from roof tops to first-floor windows like black skeletons, and women leaned out of open windows to watch the crowded streets below. Children laughed or squabbled at their play, old people sat on dilapidated chairs in doorways that led to apartments over stores, young couples strolled about aimlessly. A grubby neighborhood lay between the library and home.

Sharon scarcely saw the people and the pushcarts, the fruit stands and the omnipresent Good Humor wagon where youngsters were buying ice cream on sticks. Her mind was on Janice and her own affairs.

"I won't have to give up my classes?" She was suddenly apprehensive as well as curious.

"I should say not," Mother said emphatically. "You've found the right thing for you this summer and Monday morning you're going to the Y as you planned. I don't have to be at the library until one o'clock and Jimmy's going to take

58

the afternoon stint with the kids, until either you or Daddy get home. Everything's worked out."

"Except for Janice," Sharon finished.

"She may fit in all right." Mother's tone was hopeful rather than confident, and she plainly wasn't revealing what Aunt Agnes had said in that first letter. Sharon gave up.

It had been planned that Daddy would meet Janice at the Air Terminal, but Monday afternoon he had another appointment for a job interview and, what with classes, would be busy all day. Janice wasn't arriving until late afternoon, so when both Mother and Daddy turned to Sharon inquiringly she nodded. It looked as if it would be her assignment to meet the newcomer, and she rather enjoyed the thought of being the one to see Janice first.

Mother took Aunt Agnes' letter from the desk and read part of it aloud:

She'll be with our friends Mr. and Mrs. Phillips and their son, Ed. You can't miss Ed because he is six feet three and very thin and wears heavy glasses. Janice will wear a navy blue dress with white pin dots, a navy hat, very small, and she'll carry a white all-purpose coat which is weatherproofed in case it rains and quite right if it doesn't. She has two white leather bags. They'll go directly to the Northwest Airlines window and you can meet them there. The Phillipses will be in New York only a day or two before sailing for Amsterdam.

Sharon didn't know whether she was more excited about her own plans or meeting Janice when she left the house that Monday morning. First there was the swimming. She was eager to let Miss Moore know she was joining her group. The young instructor was standing at the edge of the pool, greeting each girl cheerfully when Sharon came in.

59

"Barbara! Good for you!"

"Liz! Nice to see you."

"Sharon! Not for real?"

"The works," Sharon told her.

"That does it! Jump in, all of you, and let me see **you** float."

Miss Moore had the girls in a semblance of formation before the hour was over. They couldn't hold a circle very well, since the two beginners didn't know how to float, and even after she had them on their backs and breathing properly they couldn't keep direction. It was a satisfactory start, though.

Miss Moore stopped Sharon when she left the pool.

"Are you going right home?" she asked. "Where are you having lunch?"

"There's a sandwich shop across the street," Sharon answered. "I thought I'd have a bite there and be back in time for my typing class. The cafeteria here seems to be closed for vacation."

"Were you meeting anyone special?" Miss Moore asked. "Could you have lunch with me?"

Sharon was glad she wasn't meeting anyone. To have lunch with Miss Moore was unexpected and it made her feel pleasantly singled out.

"Meet me in the lobby," Miss Moore said. "I won't be long."

In her bathing suit Miss Moore didn't look much older than the girls, but in a tan linen skirt and tailored green blouse she did seem more professional if not older. Sharon couldn't help thinking this luncheon was going to be really important and as soon as they had ordered Miss Moore plunged into the subject that was on her mind.

"What did you think of the group this morning? Honestly?" she asked.

"I thought they were quite good," Sharon told her. "Not as good as the Aquacade girls who finished up this spring, but just as good as we were when we started."

"That's what I thought," Miss Moore agreed. She paused while the waitress set their sandwiches and milk on the table.

"If we were to try an Aquacade, do you think Liz could take Debby's place in center?"

"Liz is a good swimmer but she hasn't had any experience in a show," Sharon said. "We wouldn't have a whole year to practice, either."

Miss Moore looked at her sandwich thoughtfully.

"After three or four more sessions maybe we'll know better whether we've got the material," she said. "If we have, would you take the lead role and help with the beginners? There isn't any budget to pay for an assistant in the summer, so I can't offer you a job with pay. Something could develop later on, though. Maybe next fall."

Sharon could scarcely believe her ears. Pay or no pay, she would love to help Miss Moore. She agreed at once.

"I won't say a thing to the Director about trying for a big final program that could be open to the public. Not until we see how it goes," Miss Moore went on. "We'll keep this confidential. But you watch the girls and help with those two beginners, and we'll talk it over after each of the next classes."

"There's nothing I'd rather do." Sharon beamed. "I'll do anything I can."

"Then let's plan on lunch again Friday. I'd rather not talk about it around the building. I'd hate to have the word get around that I'd started something I couldn't finish."

Sharon wanted to hug Miss Moore for asking her to help. She felt sure the group could develop and put on an Aquacade successfully. More than ever she wanted to see Miss Moore do well in her first real job at the Y.

Sharon arrived at the typing room early. It was just like any other classroom, with green walls, blackboards on one side, a bulletin board and drinking fountain. Six dark-stained oak desks stretched across the room, each with a typewriter, and behind them other rows of desks and machines. There were forty-eight typewriters in all and they didn't look as frisky as the drawing on the announcement. Their unlettered keys were quite formidable, in fact. On the wall above the instructor's desk a large yellow poster diagrammed the keyboard, the letters and numbers and punctuation marks emblazoned in different colors on black circles.

For a moment Sharon sat at one of the desks, looking from the marked chart on the wall to the blank keys before her. Hesitantly she touched the machine. The case was rough, but the keys were smooth and satin-soft to her finger tips. Learning to type shouldn't be too difficult, she assured herself, especially if the chart remained in sight on the wall.

Her mind returned to Miss Moore and the Aquacade, and she walked to the open window at the back of the room. The classrooms of the Ballard School were high above the street but the din of traffic could still be heard, and the smothered roar of the subway trains, a policeman's shrill whistle and honking horns mingled with the steady hum of a large electric fan that cooled the room.

On one side of Lexington Avenue, gaunt construction framework for a new building rose, black against the blue of the summer sky. On the other side, the spire of St. Peter's Lutheran Church towered. The roof of a light brick apartment building bristled with green shrubbery, and small trees on the terrace moved lazily in the summer breeze. Rows of blue awnings shaded red and green porch furniture on those roof gardens high above Manhattan's noisy, crowded midtown streets. It was a view Sharon had not seen before. Even the neon signs on the restaurant, the stationery store, and the florist's shop looked different from this height.

"Good afternoon!"

A man's voice startled her. She had expected the typing instructor to be a woman, but the young man in a white shirt and dark blue trousers definitely was the instructor. He dropped a brief case on the desk and smiled at her.

"I'm Mr. Bassett," he said. "If I were you I'd grab this desk where you get the full benefit of the fan. It's likely to be warm here before the summer's over, and in another minute you're not going to have any choice."

He was right. In another minute he was giving crisp instructions to a room full of girls, all about Sharon's age, all dressed in simple blouses and skirts and wearing sandals or flats.

Mr. Bassett wasted no time. By the end of the hour keys were clicking slowly and jerkily, space bars banged, signal bells rang.

"It will take you several days to learn the letters. Then we'll tackle the numbers, and by the end of the week you're going to be typing simple sentences."

He didn't say "if" or "maybe." He looked as though he

63

meant they all would really learn and he kept everyone busy.

A-s-d-f. Those were the left-hand starting keys, and *;-l-k-j* were the right-hand keys. The symbols were imprinted on Sharon's mind by the time the session was over. She hadn't even thought of the Aquacade or Janice for an hour and a half. It had been an exciting class period, and Sharon felt almost breathless. She hadn't expected this summer to be any fun at all, but here at the close of the first lesson she was eager for her next day at the Y. She'd ask Daddy if she could practice on his machine. If she kept her eyes off the keyboard it wouldn't be cheating, even though Daddy's keys were plainly marked.

There was plenty of time to take the bus down Lexington Avenue to Thirty-eighth Street and walk across to the Air Terminal. Again Sharon wondered what Janice would do for three or four weeks, practically alone in New York.

The vast terminal building was a fascinating place. Booths of the major airlines circled the room, and the highly polished benches were filled with well-dressed people, many chattering in foreign tongues. It was hard to think or plan for Janice with loudspeakers announcing the departure of buses for La Guardia or Idlewild and flights to Mexico City, London, Paris.

Sharon saw her cousin almost as soon as she came into the building. She was walking with a tall young man who must be Ed Phillips, and behind them came Ed's parents. Sharon took in every detail of the girl's walk and dress and appearance and found herself clutching her little red purse with growing nervousness.

Why hadn't she thought Janice might be like this!

Janice Ross was what Debby Blackwell tried to be when

64

she was her most sophisticated. Janice really was poised and self-assured. Her hair, black as Sharon's, was cut and set in the very latest fashion. There wasn't a careless curl peeping out anywhere from beneath her smart, dark-blue hat. She wore the right amount of make-up, and except for lips that drooped too much her features were all good. She wasn't a tall girl—a short size twelve, Sharon judged. She had been traveling all afternoon, but her dress was crisp and unwrinkled, her white gloves immaculate. Ed, loose-jointed and gangling, carried her coat.

One glance and Sharon was sure Janice was not interested in Ed. He was someone who happened to be along and so might carry her coat. She would expect him to get her bags and he would. She was talking to him with an air of pleasant detachment while her eyes took in the room. Other arriving tourists stopped and looked from one big sign on the walls to another: *Trans-World Airways, Pan American Airways, BOAC, Air France*. Janice was seeing it all without staring. One would have thought she arrived in New York by plane every day in the week.

What were the Heaths going to do with Janice Ross?

Janice didn't give Sharon a glance when she reached the booth where they were to meet. She was expecting Daddy, of course. For a few minutes Sharon sat still, trying to think of what to say and how to say it without showing that she was half afraid of this older cousin. Sharon hadn't even dressed for the occasion. She could have worn something beside a red cotton skirt and a sleeveless white blouse, even though the day was hot. She hadn't even thought of gloves or a hat. Now she realized her red-and-white outfit was decidedly schoolgirlish.

There wasn't anything to do about it now. She couldn't put off her meeting with Janice. Inwardly she squared her shoulders and got up.

"You're Janice Ross, aren't you?" she heard herself saying. "I'm Sharon Heath. Daddy couldn't come to meet you so I'm here."

"Sharon! I thought I'd remember you, but you've changed a lot."

Janice smiled fleetingly, then introduced Sharon to the Phillips family. Sharon liked Ed and Mr. Phillips immediately, but Mrs. Phillips was a middle-aged Janice, looking exactly like an advertisement in a high-fashion magazine.

"You had a nice day for the trip," Sharon said. "Was it a smooth flight?" What was there to say to these people?

They spoke pleasantly about the trip while Mr. Phillips led the way to the taxi stand on the floor below. Sharon knew she was being measured with each casual glance. Quite unexpectedly Janice turned to her with a friendly smile.

"Have you anything planned for tonight?" she asked. "I mean has Aunt Ardith planned anything for either of us?"

"Why no," Sharon answered. She didn't know what Janice had expected. Probably they should have planned something.

"Then it would be nice if you got theater tickets for us too, Sharon and me," Janice said to Mrs. Phillips. "I don't know what Sharon's seen, of course. Not everything, I hope." She looked inquiringly at Sharon.

Sharon didn't know whether to be pleased or not. It was nice that Janice included her in the plans for the evening, and she hadn't seen a Broadway show for a long time, but what was this going to cost? Sharon was sure that Janice and the Phillipses wouldn't buy balcony seats, and she had every cent of her July allowance committed. Besides, what was Mother going to think?

"I'll see what we can get," Mrs. Phillips told the girls. "Dad always stops at the Plaza and they can usually get what we want. It may not be possible to see 'Lorraine,' but we can certainly get something."

"Is there anything you'd particularly recommend?" Janice asked Sharon. "What have you already seen?"

The questions were embarrassing. Sharon tried to remember what the *New Yorker* had said about the current shows, realizing that these people probably knew more about them than she. If they read the theater magazines regularly, they did.

"The critics agreed on 'Lorraine,'" Sharon ventured. She was sure of that. "Whatever you can get will be all right."

"I suppose we all read the same reviews by the same critics," Mrs. Phillips said. "The *Times,* the *New Yorker.* But until you've seen a play you don't really know."

"And your friends who have seen them are just like the critics," Sharon said bravely. "You can't rely upon some other person's judgment."

It was a remark she had heard Debby make, and Debby probably was quoting her father. Sharon felt like a "phony," but she was ill at ease with Mrs. Phillips and Janice.

Mr. Phillips touched his wife's elbow when a boy finished loading their luggage into the two taxis he had ordered.

"I'll call you as soon as we get the tickets," Mrs. Phillips said and kissed Janice lightly on the cheek. "It will be nice to have Janice's little cousin along tonight." She smiled pleasantly, and Mr. Phillips and Ed, who had been standing

67

patiently beside the two taxis, smiled too. Then they all said good-by, and Sharon gave the driver her address and settled back self-consciously.

"You live in the Village, don't you?" Janice asked. "I suppose the Dos Passoses and Theodore Dreisers and Rockwell Kents of tomorrow are just unknown people who live next door to you."

Once more Sharon scrambled mentally for the right answer.

"I guess that's right," she said. "The man in the other apartment in our house is writing a book. We hear him typing all the time. Who knows?"

It was what Janice wanted to hear. "Will I meet him?" she asked. "Tomorrow his book may be a best seller, and then a movie and a TV play. Who does know? Tomorrow the moon."

"Do you ever see the Roy Blackwell show?" Sharon went on. "The Blackwells live just a few blocks from our house and Debby's one of my friends. She's been on her father's show once or twice. But you'd know that."

Trading on her acquaintance with Debby wasn't natural for Sharon, but there was almost an obligation to make New York the glamorous place Janice was expecting. *The Villager* regularly listed important people who had taken up residence in the Washington Square neighborhood, and Debby always read those notes with interest. Sharon wondered if the last issue of the paper was around the house somewhere. She'd have to look at it when it came this week.

Janice paid the taxi fare when they reached home, and Sharon was reassured about the theater tickets almost at once, for as soon as she had met the family Janice announced that Mr. and Mrs. Phillips were taking them to the theater that evening, and she hoped it would be all right with Aunt Ardith.

"I think it's lovely of the Phillipses," Mother said. "They didn't need to include Sharon in the theater party, but it's very nice that they did."

"Don't worry about the Phillipses," Janice said lightly. "Mr. Phillips invented something and now every time an automobile rolls off an assembly line in Detroit he gets a nice fat check!"

"Have you known them long?" Mother asked, leading the way to Sharon's room while Daddy followed with the two white leather bags.

"Since before they made all this wonderful money," Janice answered. "Mr. Phillips and Dad stayed good friends, so Mrs. Phillips had to keep on knowing us."

There was a tinge of bitterness in Janice's laugh.

"Ed seemed all right," Sharon suggested. "He was pretty quiet. He didn't say anything, did he?"

"He never does. I never knew him to even try to be entertaining," Janice told her.

Daddy set Janice's bags down, glanced at her briefly, and left Mother with the two girls in Sharon's little bedroom. Nancy and Cathy had trailed along and were watching Janice's every move from the hall. Three people, two bags, two youngsters in the doorway, then Jato tearing upstairs and bouncing in to get acquainted with the newcomer—it was all very congested and certainly much different from the home life of Janice's friends, the Phillips family.

What was Janice expecting in these next few weeks? Broadway shows, celebrities, excitement, of course. Sharon glanced at her mother, who was helping unpack the two white bags. The pretty dresses that were being transferred to Sharon's closet showed plainly what Janice had in mind. Not a play suit or a pair of dungarees in the lot! If Mother had anticipated this, no wonder she hadn't been enthusiastic about their visitor. The situation was really quite overwhelming. What were they going to do?

Then, with a sudden impulsive gesture, Janice relaxed. She put her arms around Sharon and hugged her.

"We're going to have a wonderful time," she said. "My first visit to New York! My first night on Broadway!"

CHAPTER SIX

"PICKING UP THE TAB"

DINNER was a strained and uncomfortable meal, although Mother and Daddy did their best to make Janice feel welcome and one of the family. Jimmy bolted his food and couldn't wait to get out of the house, even though Janice was particularly nice to him. Nancy and Cathy giggled whenever anything was said to them, and Sharon's mind was on what she should wear that evening.

Janice was thinking of clothes, too, and as soon as dinner was over she went upstairs to bathe and dress without offering to help with the work in the kitchen.

"She might have offered," Sharon whispered to her mother while they cleared the table.

"I'm afraid we'll have to accept her as she is," Mother replied. "She isn't like Marie and Debby and the girls you run around with. She's older, you know. A year in college . . .

and I guess being an only child . . . anyway, she's our paying guest and she came to New York to have a good time."

It was the kind of good time Janice had in mind that bothered Sharon. When she got upstairs, the bed was draped with dresses and Janice's filmy lingerie practically covered the one little chair. There was no place to sit except the stool at the dressing table.

Janice was holding up a pale green wash silk and surveying it critically.

"I'll have to press this, I guess," she said. "Where do you press?"

"Downstairs in the kitchen," Sharon told her. "Mother'll show you."

She was glad to have Janice out of the room while she got ready, and she was very glad Janice had selected that dress. It was as right for the theater as the simple blue silk with pearl trimming which was all Sharon had to wear.

She should have known that Janice would not over-dress and that she would nevertheless be dramatic. A nice little figure in a soft green dress, a pretty face framed by black curls, and earrings that were a cluster of small brilliants, jade and dots of jet—people would look at Janice more than once that evening.

Even Jimmy stopped his conversation long enough to stare at her when the two girls passed Pop's store on their way to the bus.

"Listen, you! Rube Marquard won nineteen consecutive games. . . ." It was the argumentative tone Sharon knew so well.

"Hello, Jimmy," Janice said sweetly and smiled at him.

Jimmy gulped a "hello" and turned, red-faced, back to the

crowd of boys who were staring at Janice, too. Sharon held her breath until they were safely beyond Pop's place. It would be awful if Jimmy or any of his friends should whistle.

"The youngsters really should be in camp," Janice observed. "Mother told me your father's teaching this summer. It's too bad the kids can't go to camp."

Sharon didn't want to discuss the family situation with Janice. "What does your father do?" she asked. "I can't remember, if anyone ever told me."

"He's in charge of a bunch of salesmen for one of Milwaukee's big packing houses," Janice said. "We get along, though he'll never be rich or famous. Look, if you know any of the people we see and they're *anybody*, point them out to me."

"We aren't likely to see any celebrities on the Sixth Avenue bus," Sharon said, signaling the approaching bus driver to stop.

"Does the bus go right to the Plaza?" Janice asked after they had lurched to a seat at the back, past people standing in the aisle. "Couldn't we get off somewhere before we get there and take a taxi? The Phillipses would never ride a bus."

"The bus doesn't go right to the Plaza," Sharon explained. "It stops about a block away. Everybody in New York rides buses and subways unless they're millionaires, practically."

Janice wasn't convinced. "I don't know . . . the Plaza . . . I think we should arrive in a taxi."

"Unless they're waiting on the steps they'll never know how we got there," Sharon insisted. She didn't want to spend her dwindling allowance to help pay a taxi fare. "Would they be horrified if they did see us walking from the corner?"

Janice didn't really frown, but the corners of her mouth drooped. "I suppose not. It's a nice night," she admitted.

Sharon pointed out the major landmarks on the trip up to Central Park South and Janice glanced at the buildings with a mild show of interest. Macy's and Gimbel's were not the places she had in mind for shopping, Sharon gathered.

At Fifty-seventh Street Janice suddenly jumped from her seat. "Isn't the Plaza at Fifty-ninth Street? Let's get off here."

She hurried to the exit, Sharon following, and stepped down just before the doors were ready to close. With a quick sidewise step she was on the street, and then she cried out in sudden pain.

"Janice! What's the matter?"

"Oh, my ankle!" Janice's face turned white and her lips tightened, and for a moment Sharon thought she was going to faint. She put her arm around her cousin's waist to help her from the pavement to the sidewalk.

"Can you step on it?"

Janice put her weight cautiously on her foot. "Yes . . . yes, it isn't broken. Maybe not even sprained." She tested it carefully and the color began to come back to her face. "I guess I just hurt it. Let's find a drugstore and buy some aspirin."

"Don't you think we should go home?"

"Don't be ridic!" Janice sounded almost cross. "And don't say anything about it to the Phillipses. I certainly don't want Ed to think I fell on my face the first day I got to New York."

Janice bought aspirin and an ankle bandage which she stuffed into her purse. At the soda fountain she got water and took two tablets.

"Don't tell Aunt Ardith either," she cautioned while they walked slowly to the Plaza. "She'd probably tell Mom and I don't want Mom worrying about me right away. She's worried enough already, and there's more to come."

Sharon looked at her in surprise. "What do you mean, 'more to come'?"

"I'll tell you later. Aren't we almost there?"

Sharon was sure that Janice's ankle was paining her, and she was glad when they reached the hotel. Whenever she had thought of the place she had pictured it as ultra-modern, and the old-fashioned lobby with its gleaming white marble was not what she had expected. Neither had she expected the Phillipses to be in evening clothes when they came to the lobby in response to Janice's phone call. Mrs. Phillips wore a beige evening dress, and although it was warm she carried a mink stole. Her necklace and bracelet were real diamonds, Sharon decided.

"We got 'Lorraine,'" Mrs. Phillips said brightly. "I'm so glad, for I think you girls will enjoy it. It's supposed to be good theater. I guess Daddy and Ed will like it as well as anything."

Ed, as usual, had little to say, but Mr. Phillips assured his wife he always liked the theater no matter how bad it was, and he signaled the doorman to call a cab for them.

It was a relief to Sharon to know that Janice would not have to do any more walking. She wondered, while she listened to comments about the famous Broadway signs, how long it would be before the aspirin took effect.

75

"I like the one where smoke comes out of a pipe," Mr. Phillips told the girls and didn't hesitate to stretch his neck and look. The white lights on the theater marquees were gleaming now, and blocks and blocks of animated signs, crowded together, formed an avenue of moving, flashing, gaudily colored display.

"I want to see the waterfall," Janice announced, so Mr. Phillips had the cab driver go slowly past the sign. It was as Sharon remembered it, high above the street, with tons of water endlessly bubbling over a cement precipice.

There was the usual slow-moving crowd outside the theater, so Janice didn't have to walk fast or far. Once or twice Sharon looked at her questioningly, but not until they were seated did Janice give her an encouraging smile.

Sharon had never seen a play from the fifth-row center before. Many people in the select seats around them were in evening dress. There was more of the feeling of the theater, the lure and glamour of sequins and satin and exotic make-up, than she had sensed from the balcony, where she had always sat before. "Lorraine" was a musical comedy with a strong thread of plot, and Sharon forgot to worry about Janice until between acts, when her cousin decided not to go to the lobby for a breath of air.

"I guess I'll just stay here," Janice said when Ed suggested going for an orange drink. She didn't look at Sharon.

Sharon was completely unprepared, too, for the after-theater supper which was part of the Phillipses' plans. A roof garden atop one of the city's big hotels had been selected for their little snack.

"I'll have to call Mother," Sharon said quietly. "Don't you think we'd better go home?"

76

"Don't be ridic!" Janice said again. "We'll call her from the hotel if you think we should."

Mrs. Phillips agreed that they should call and said she would talk to Mother, too. "If all three of us talk to her I'm sure she'll know you girls are safe," Mrs. Phillips said. "We'll put you in a cab promptly at one o'clock and start you home."

Sharon never forgot that night. It was like a movie, where everything happened to somebody else. In the powder room, before they went to the roof garden, Janice took more aspirin, with a sorry look at her slightly swollen ankle. She also took a lovely bracelet from her purse and put it on. She must have thought it too elaborate for the theater.

"Rhinestones," she smiled. "All that glitters isn't 'a girl's best friend.'" Her voice was cheerful, and her look warned Sharon again not to mention the accident.

From the lobby they took an elevator directly to the roof, and when Mr. Phillips gave his name to the headwaiter they were taken to a reserved table at once.

Crystal chandeliers picked up the rose and gold of walls and draperies and the myriad colors of the dancers' gowns. In brocades, taffetas and swirling net the ladies shimmered from hair ornaments to evening slippers. The room was air-conditioned, and Mrs. Phillips had need for her mink wrap. Mr. Phillips thoughtfully placed it around her shoulders.

"We'll have to dance or freeze to death," he observed and gave the order to the waiter. "Seven-Up for the little ladies and champagne cocktails for three." Then he smiled at his wife and offered Janice his arm.

Sharon couldn't help glancing at the ankle when Janice went out onto the dance floor, but Ed was extending his hand to her and she knew she musn't stare. He danced to one

77

of the windows which was not draped, and stopped, moving easily with the music, while Sharon looked at the panorama of skyscrapers, windows lighted hit-or-miss, etched black against a sky rose-tinted from the reflected garish street lights far below. This was New York, where she had lived all her life, but she had never seen it like this before. It was the New York Janice had anticipated and did not intend to miss.

Janice came to life and laughed and sparkled all evening. She even tried to flirt with Ed and coaxed him to come out of his shell. Without looking at the oversized menu she ordered curried shrimp. Sharon, who had been floundering through dozens of items of food, aghast at the prices, decided to make the same selection. Whatever Janice did would be right.

Sharon danced with Mr. Phillips and again with Ed before their supper came. They had scarcely finished when Mrs. Phillips reminded them of their promise to Mother, and Mr. Phillips took them all back to the lobby. Once more he had the doorman summon cabs.

Janice, flushed and happy, launched into plans for the next day while Sharon was still giving the driver her address.

"The Phillipses are 'going tourist' tomorrow and do the Statue of Liberty, and have lunch at the St. Moritz sidewalk café, and take the excursion boat around Manhattan Island in the late afternoon. We'll have a swell time."

"But your ankle?" Sharon asked.

"It's not broken," Janice scoffed. "I'll put the bandage on it tonight and hold it down. I just hope your mother doesn't notice it. We've got to have fun while we can."

"We?" Sharon asked. "The Phillipses didn't invite me."

"Well, I latched on for both of us," Janice announced. "No sense in spending my allowance while they're around to pick up the tab."

Sharon didn't like the sound of that. "Look, Janice, I'm not going. They probably like to have you along to pep Ed up, but they don't know me and I'm not going to have them spend any more money on me."

"Oh, Sharon!" Janice sounded disgusted. "This little supper tonight didn't cost fifty bucks, with us drinking Seven-Up. I've seen old B.J. spend five hundred dollars on an evening."

"Five hundred dollars!" Sharon couldn't believe it.

"Anything they spend on me now—well, I'd say it's the least they can do!"

There was bitterness in Janice's voice when she said it, but Sharon could not question her then. The cab had stopped in front of their house and Janice got out slowly. She started up the steps without offering to pay the driver.

Sharon had no idea what the fare would be, and she turned to the man with considerable concern. Clearly it was up to her to "pick up the tab" this time. The driver, however, shook his head.

" 'Old B.J.' paid for this too," he assured her. "Hurry along, Miss. I'll wait until you're safe inside."

Janice was removing her shoes when Sharon caught up with her. "Let's not wake your mother if we can help it," she whispered.

From the cabinet in the bathroom Sharon took a bottle of liniment and, back in the bedroom, she rubbed it gently on Janice's swollen ankle. She wished she knew what Janice had meant by that reference to the Phillipses, but she didn't

79

know how to ask the question. She didn't have to ask it, as it happened.

"How much has your mother told you about me?" Janice asked in a low voice, sitting on the bed and toying with the ankle bandage.

"Not much," Sharon told her. "I hardly remembered you, to tell the truth."

Janice drew a long breath. "Well, I know Mother told Aunt Ardith everything, so you may as well know it. I'll tell you the whole story, too—the part even Mother doesn't know —if you'll promise to keep it to yourself until I get around to telling her. Promise?"

Sharon hesitated. "You *are* going to tell her?" she asked.

"Yes, of course I'm going to tell her."

"All right," Sharon promised.

"I guess there isn't anything particularly unusual about it," Janice began. "Just a broken engagement. I met the boy through Ed Phillips. We all were going to the University of Wisconsin last year and before Christmas I announced my engagement at a sorority house party. So there was much ado there, and back home in Milwaukee, with the Phillipses giving big parties and my picture in the papers. Showers and stuff. You know. When we went back to Madison I thought everything was lovely at first, but little by little I began to feel something was wrong. When spring vacation came and he didn't say anything about coming home to visit me, I knew it."

Janice stopped and slipped the ankle bandage into place.

"To make a long story short, his folks objected. They said we were much too young and that by the time we were twenty-five we'd both be sorry. And the campus full of mar-

80

ried students! I guess they really put the bee on him. He wrote me a letter and gave it to Ed to deliver, so I'd have a shoulder to weep on. And he didn't come back to Madison. Thank heavens for that!"

"Oh, Janice!" Sharon sympathized. "That's about the worst thing that can happen to a girl. I can't imagine how anyone could do a thing like that."

"Well, he could and did!" Janice said. "I'm the one who had to send back the gifts and do the explaining. I'm the one who was rejected. Mother and Dad made me go back to college and finish out the year, but they can't make me go next year. I'm eighteen, and they can't make me."

She took the rhinestone bracelet from her wrist and threw it down on the bed between them.

"I'm not going back to Milwaukee, Sharon," she whispered. "I'm going to stay right here in New York!"

CHAPTER SEVEN

A MATTER OF VALUES

For a moment Sharon sat beside her cousin in silence. When the full significance of Janice's confidence came to her, she felt tricked and resentful. What was Mother going to think when she learned of this plan and of Sharon's unthinking promise to keep it secret? Must she share her room and her home, perhaps, all summer, with this cousin whom she did not understand and almost disliked?

In the dressing-table mirror across the room Sharon saw her own face, a picture of dismay; saw Janice, absorbed in her own thoughts, rubbing her ankle. How could two cousins, so near the same age and daughters of twin sisters, be so different? Except for Sharon's upturned nose they even looked quite a bit alike, she suddenly realized. The thought was distasteful. She got up and began to undress.

"When are you going to tell your mother?" she asked in a hushed voice. "When are you going to tell my mother?"

"As soon as I get a job," Janice answered. "I'll start looking after the Phillipses leave. I hope I can get something before the time Mom expects me to come home. Before she and Aunt Ardith get suspicious. I'd like to have everything settled before I tell them. A place to live and everything. I know I can't stay here with you too long . . . this little room! So maybe you can help me look."

Help Janice look for a job, too! How could she?

"What are you going to do?" Sharon asked. "What do you know how to do?"

Janice looked from her foot to her reflection in the mirror. Slowly she unzipped her dress and let it slide down over her smooth shoulders.

"What about modeling?" she asked. "I've had a little training. Dancing school and gym when I was a kid. That taught me something."

Stepping out of her dress, Sharon looked at Janice appraisingly. She was pretty and she wore clothes with sophisticated assurance, but Sharon didn't know what Mother would think of modeling as an occupation.

"I don't know anything about modeling," Sharon told her. "I wouldn't know how to begin to look for such a job."

She had a feeling of relief after she had said it. She simply couldn't help with this surreptitious plan.

Janice's blue eyes were questioning.

"I guess probably you couldn't," she said at last. "I keep forgetting you're only sixteen. Because you live in New York . . . because you don't seem like a kid. . . . Don't think any more about it. I'll tell our mothers just as soon as I can. I guess I shouldn't have said anything about it."

Sharon couldn't think of anything to say, nor could she

84

forget it. Long after the lights were out and Janice was breathing evenly, Sharon lay awake thinking about this night: the theater, the supper club, the evening of dancing and dining. Then Janice and these secret plans. Why couldn't she have been dancing with Brad—no problems and no intrigue? Dancing with Brad in that elegant rose room with the glistening chandeliers and smooth music!

Sharon didn't think she had been asleep at all when the aroma of toast and coffee roused her. She sat up and swung out of bed, then stopped, remembering what was ahead of her. Mother would be eager to know all about what had happened and she couldn't tell the most important part. She looked at Janice still sleeping, and with a sigh of resignation went to the bathroom to shower and dress.

Daddy and the youngsters had finished breakfast when Sharon got downstairs, and Mother, who had been reading the paper, put more bread into the toaster when Sharon came into the dining room. In green slacks and a white blouse Mother looked young and pretty and very understanding to Sharon.

"Did you have a wonderful time?" she asked. She was smiling, expecting to hear all about it. "Begin at the beginning."

The beginning was the theater and that was easy. The roof-garden dancing and Janice's plans to see New York today with the Phillipses, and even the invitation for Sharon to come along, could be told.

"Did Mrs. Phillips invite you?" Mother questioned.

"I guess so. She didn't say anything to me about it, actually. It was Janice who invited me," Sharon admitted.

"What are you going to do?"

85

"I don't think I should go," Sharon said. "In fact, I don't want to and I told Janice so. Mrs. Phillips didn't say anything about meeting you either, now that I think about it."

"That's all right," Mother said quickly. "She has only a few days here and a great many things to do. We'd never see each other again. I knew what to expect from what Agnes wrote."

"What did she write?" Sharon pressed. If only Mother would tell her part of it. If there was some way Sharon could indicate that Janice had confided in her. Mother, however, didn't give Sharon the response she hoped for.

"I think you're learning, little by little, about Janice," Mother said. "Seeing New York with the Phillipses isn't the best thing that could happen to her, although they invited her and Aunt Agnes couldn't find any excuse for saying no. There isn't any reason why you and I should try to change her plans now, either, but Janice has become too impressed by money and what it can buy."

"Well, money is important!" Sharon agreed with Janice on that point.

"Not so important as what people do and how they live and what they accomplish in life," Mother reminded Sharon. "I hope we can help Janice recover her sense of values while she's with us. At least make a start."

"We?" Sharon couldn't hide her surprise. "*We* change Janice?" They might as well try to reason with one of the statues in the park, Sharon thought. If Mother knew Janice's plans. . . .

"What are you going to do about this invitation, if it *is* an invitation?" Mother asked.

"I think it would be 'latching on' even if Mrs. Phillips had invited me, and I'm not going." There was no question in Sharon's mind about it.

Mother nodded. "I don't like that expression but I do agree," she said. "I have an idea Janice won't press you. Four is a nice number for a party and you'd be a fifth wheel. What I'm concerned about is the next few weeks and whether she'll fit into your summer program after her friends have sailed."

Sharon helped herself to toast. "She'll probably want dates, and I don't know any boys her age except Dick. Do you suppose we could ask him to take her out? Or maybe he has a friend at the Academy who might like to meet her—some boy from Wisconsin, maybe."

"Ask Dick," Mother proposed. "We should get in touch with him anyway and find out definitely when he graduates and what he knows about shipping out after he finishes. You've got to let Brad know so he and his mother can begin to plan for the Cape party."

Sharon groaned and moved her plate away. When she saw Dick she was going to have to tell him, too, about the lost scholarship.

"If I'm going to ask him to take Janice out or get her a date I may as well tell him the rest of the bad news," she sighed.

"Oh, Sharon! Things aren't so bad," Mother protested. "A summer in Manhattan isn't so terrible, is it? You haven't had such a bad week, have you?"

There was no denying that she had enjoyed her first sessions at the Y. There was even the hope of more active participation in the swimming program next fall. If it wasn't for all these complications!

"Why don't you take the little tote wagon and go over to

87

the Bleecker Street stands for me before you go to typing class?" Mother suggested. "I've made out the list."

Sharon went, and when she returned with her load of fruit and vegetables Janice was gone. She had told Mother she wouldn't be home until after the theater that evening. Apparently her ankle had been unnoticed and unmentioned.

Janice was no problem to Sharon the rest of the week. As Mother had predicted, four made a nice party, so Sharon continued her daily typing class and went swimming on Friday without interference. She had not expected Janice to help with the Saturday work either, but she did wonder where Janice was going when again she left the house soon after breakfast.

About noon the mail carrier came with a letter from Brad, and Sharon stopped everything to sit on the front steps and tear the envelope open.

"Oh, Mother! The boat!" Sharon called. "He's sent pictures of their wonderful new cruising yacht!"

Mother came to the door and after a hasty look at the snapshots, Sharon handed them to her and began reading the letter.

Dear Sharon,

Well, here she is and what a honey! All she needs is you on deck. Take a look at the name. It shows up best on the one with Dad at the back. . . .

"Mother, quick! Let me see the pictures again," Sharon said, reaching for them. "What did they name it?"

Mother was smiling when she handed the snapshots back. The one on top was the one Brad had mentioned. Though the lettering was hazy, it was clear enough to read: *Rose of*

Sharon. Sharon didn't try to hide her pleasure. She began reading aloud:

It's white with a rose-colored trim. That's why we gave it that name, of course. It sleeps eight, with four bunks letting down like upper berths on a Pullman. The galley is about the size of your broom closet but you'd be surprised how much storage space there is in the cupboards and lockers and under the bunks. We could cruise a month without going into port for food.

The drawers are lined with special paper to keep clothes from getting moldy and the lockers have racks to hold the dishes when the boat rolls. They wouldn't break if they fell, for they're of wood and if they went overboard we could just dive in and get them, all washed and ready to put away. . . .

Sharon turned a page. There were sketches showing the location of everything, including cockpit, motor, and rudder, and the interior of the cabin.

We took the record player out yesterday and cruised all day, then we rode at anchor last night. You've no idea how pretty the music sounded out on the water. Do you want to know the record I played most? It's on the top of The Sharon's hit parade. "Wish You Were Here."

"Wish you were here." Popular music, and Brad never chose popular albums. Sharon read that last sentence with misty eyelashes. She looked at the pictures and imagined the glorious time ahead when they celebrated Dick's graduation with Brad at the Cape. She stuffed the letter in the pocket of her blue jeans, and more than once during her morning household chores she took it out to re-read that final paragraph. When her work was done she phoned Marie and read the letter to her.

"I can't wait to see the pictures," Marie said. "What are you doing tomorrow?"

It was a tactful way of telling Sharon that she had a date that evening, but Sharon didn't mind.

"What's to do that doesn't cost money?" she asked.

"Nothing but go over to the park. Want to meet me around two-thirty? Maybe Russell Moore'll be along. He hasn't left town yet. You remember Russell, don't you?"

"Long ago I gave up trying to remember," Sharon told her. "You go through boy friends the way I go through my allowance. I'll meet you, though. Somewhere around the big cement circle, say?"

"On the side nearest Washington Arch. Don't forget to bring the pictures."

"I'm likely to forget all about them," Sharon mocked.

She spent the evening writing two letters, a long one to Brad and a short one to Dick. Writing to Brad was easy, for she had a great deal to tell him. Writing to Dick was more difficult, and Sharon made several tries before she was satisfied that her letter didn't sound as though she wanted sympathy or was trying to be a brave, noble girl.

Dear Dick,

I know you're going to be surprised at this letter, but these are changing times. Dad's teaching summer school and I'm swimming at the Y instead of up at camp. I have a charming house guest on my hands for the next two or three weeks, too. Perhaps you recall hearing about my cousin Janice Ross who lives in Milwaukee. She's the same relation to me as you, only on Mother's side.

Which brings me to Point Number One of this letter. Would you or any of the boys at the Academy have the time, inclination, and necessary cabbage for a date with a very pretty but

slightly-on-the-expensive-side girl? Mother'll have a nice dinner here, so you can get acquainted before you take her out.
Then all you'd have to invest would be the cost of the rest of the
evening. You can call me and let me know. It's easier for you to
call than for me to get you located, out on those expansive old
Chrysler acres, or on the Sound or what-not.

When you come in you can tell me all the facts about graduation so we can begin making definite plans for Our Week up on
the Cape with the Johnsons. And I'll tell you all about how I
am not going to college in Colorado next year!

Your affectionate cousin,
Sharon

Sharon felt a little lonely while she walked to the mailbox
on Waverly Place to post her letters. It was her first Saturday
night of the summer in town, and there was nothing to do and
no one to do it with. She stopped at Pop's store on the way
home and bought a popsicle. No one there whom she knew,
either. She let each cool bite melt in her mouth and trickle
slowly down her throat. She might as well go home and
watch television with the kids, only it was so hot to stay
inside. Perhaps she'd take a shower and put on her pajama-
shorties and then watch television.

She thought of the pool at the Y and her swimming group
and typing class. Was any of it going to lead to anything, or
was it just a way to put in this long, hot summer? She had
meant to talk to the guidance counselor about typing, but so
far she hadn't done it. Should she ask about modeling too? It
wouldn't be betraying her promise if she didn't mention her
cousin's name.

Where was Janice tonight, she wondered, and thought of
the glamorous places she had heard Debby mention. Places
Sharon had never seen or thought about seriously. Strange

that her cousin from Milwaukee should know more about New York's glittering cafés and night clubs than she, who had always lived here.

Sharon sat down on her own front steps and finished her popsicle. Inside she heard the music of a television program and from adjoining apartments came the subdued tones of other programs and other songs. Out on the waters off Cape Cod there was music too, she thought. Brad's letter was still in her pocket. Her fingers closed around the envelope tightly.

CHAPTER EIGHT

THE PARK AND SUNDAY COPS

SHARON hadn't expected to have Janice with her when she met Marie and Russell the next day. She had assumed that the Phillipses would have elaborate plans for Sunday, but when she stretched and got out of bed that morning Janice unexpectedly sat up too.

"What's on for today?" she asked, rubbing her eyes.

"Nothing. Church. I'm meeting Marie after dinner," Sharon said. "She's the artist friend I think I told you about." Then, after a moment's hesitation, "Want to come along? There isn't much of anything to do." Inwardly Sharon began to dread the afternoon. Loafing in the park was hardly the thing for Janice.

"Anything's better than the museums," she heard Janice saying. "Besides, Ed's getting awfully boring."

Sharon could imagine that Ed was bored too, and not good company.

"Marie knows a couple of older fellows," Sharon suggested. "They might be with her. I've invited Dick Mendendahl in to meet you. Maybe you'll like him."

"Don't worry about me," Janice said, getting out of bed. "Who's going to shower first, you or me? You sure have hot nights in New York."

Hot days too, Sharon thought. By afternoon the city would be torrid.

Trees gave welcome shade to most of the benches in Washington Square Park, but the big cement circle in the center shimmered and baked in the sun. It had been built as a wading pool, but Sharon couldn't remember when the city had last turned the water on, nor why it had been drained. Now it was a gathering place for young people who sat on the rounded rim with their favorite group of musicians and sang and talked and sang again. Two or three stringed instruments and a homemade drum fashioned from a small washtub supplied the music for most of the groups. Anyone could sing, although older people generally stood back and watched while interested tourists took pictures endlessly.

"You mean people sit out there in that lethal sun and sing on a day like this?" Janice gasped as they sauntered toward the circle. Janice had kept on the silk dress she had worn to church, but Sharon had changed into her coolest white cotton blouse and aqua skirt.

"I told you to put on something cool," Sharon reminded her. "There's one group over in the shade by the statue of Alexander Lyman Holly. I don't recognize them. Maybe they're new."

"Who's Alexander Lyman Holly?"

"I don't know. He had something to do with the manufacture of steel, and it says the engineers of two hemispheres erected the statue," Sharon told her. "Let's go over and see what's going on."

Two young couples, one with a baby about six months old, had grouped themselves on the grass at the base of the statue. One man strummed a banjo, the other a guitar, and they were singing old Irish folk songs in low voices. The tempo was slow, the songs lamentations, and Sharon didn't know the one they were singing:

When the robins nest agen
  And the flowers are in bloom
When the Springtime's sunny smile seems to banish all sorrow
    and gloom;
  Then me bonny blue-ey'd lad, if me heart be true till then—
He promised he'll come back to me
  When the robins nest agen.

Only one person in the small group of listeners seemed to know the dirgelike melody and words. The singers weren't attracting a large following.

"We've got to meet Marie over near the arch," Sharon reminded Janice and began drifting toward the larger circle. The rim was crowded with young people and there wasn't any place to sit. Sharon and Janice stood at the edge of a group of singers crowded around four young musicians in blue jeans, shirts open at the neck, who were leading in American folk songs. They had banjos and guitars and a washtub drum and they strummed a livelier tune:

From California to New York Island
This land was made for us.

Boys and girls sang casually, stared at others in the lazy circle, suggested something else to sing and sang again.

95

Sharon had seen many of them before, but she didn't know any by name and most of them seemed not to know each other. They sang a verse or two, wandered away for a Good Humor, and came back.

"How about 'Anne Boleyn'?" a slender, dark-eyed boy asked the musicians. Sharon had seen him there before and had thought him one of the group. Today he was wearing a white sailor's hat and navy-blue shirt and trousers.

"Anne Boleyn" had endless verses. With her head under her arm, Anne came back to the court of King Henry the Eighth to create all kinds of situations. Different singers seemed to recall different verses, and Sharon suspected they made new ones up, from Sunday to Sunday, to add interest to the song and its repetitious melody.

"Hi, Sharon!" It was Marie. "You remember Russell Moore?"

Sharon recalled the fair-haired, blue-eyed boy when she saw him. He was wearing gray slacks and a light-blue shirt, and he and dark-haired Marie made an arresting couple. Sharon introduced Janice, whose smiling acknowledgment took in the situation at once. In yellow slacks, blue blouse, and without her shimmering copper jewelry, Marie looked younger than her eighteen years, and Russell not only seemed too young for Janice but was obviously interested in Marie.

Unexpectedly, the boy in the sailor hat spoke to Russell, who introduced him as Victor Basso. He was no older than the others.

"I've seen you here before, haven't I?" Victor asked Sharon. "With some other kids? A brown-haired fellow and a rather thin girl?"

"Brad Johnson and Debby Blackwell," Sharon said.

"So that's who she is! I knew I'd seen her. Now I know. On television with her dad."

"Look, kids," Janice pleaded. "Couldn't we get out of the sun before I die of third-degree burns?"

"There's a group across the circle singing Yiddish songs," Marie said. "Want to listen to them awhile? Different national groups sing, too. . . ."

"But never in the shade?" Janice persisted.

"Your neck *is* getting pink," Marie commented, and started from the scorching circle, although Sharon was sure she had expected to stay there and sing. "Want to come over to the Salmagundi Club and take a look at the black-and-white exhibition there?"

"What's the Salmagundi Club?" Janice asked.

"It's the oldest art club in the United States," Marie explained. "Some of the most distinguished American artists and architects have belonged—for instance Stanford White, who designed the Washington Arch."

Janice didn't respond, and Sharon remembered she had deserted the Phillipses to avoid going to the Metropolitan Museum.

"Let's get a Good Humor," Victor proposed and started in the opposite direction. The wagon was in the shade, and Janice looked grateful when she took the paper cup of strawberry ice cream he offered. He took a bag of peanuts from his pocket after he had finished his own ice cream and threw a handful to a swarm of gray pigeons cooing at their feet. Irridescent neck and wing feathers immediately were fluttering as pigeons from all over the park came for the food. The air was thick and noisy with the beating of hundreds of

97

descending wings, and Janice backed away. A park police officer looked at her and laughed.

"They won't bite," he joked. "Anything but food, that is."

"I've got a new motor bike my uncle just brought back from Italy," Victor suggested. If you haven't seen these Italian jobs I could get it and ride the girls around. One at a time, that is."

"It's neat all right," Russell agreed. "I've only seen one like yours."

It was something to do. They left the crowded, noisy park, Victor leading the way and walking with Janice and Sharon.

The streets south of Washington Square were not attractive. Old buildings leaned against each other and scraggly plants in broken flower pots tilted unevenly in apartment windows over stores. Bedding hung on fire escapes. Sharon wondered what sort of neighborhood Victor was taking them to and avoided looking at Janice. The delicatessens and barber shops, laundromats and cigar stores were familiar to her and to Marie and Russell, but Janice had been haunting the Plaza and Sherry-Netherland.

Sharon was relieved when Victor stopped in front of a new and streamlined building, even though the corner section was an undertaking parlor. The adjoining stores had been renovated, and above their glass and plastic fronts Venetian blinds suggested new apartments. A shining hearse, heaped with huge floral pieces, stood at the curb, and behind it a limousine was being filled with more massive blankets of flowers.

"I never saw anything like it!" Janice gasped. "Look at that one! It's like a gigantic floor lamp!"

Victor did not sense the criticism. "It's a real beaut, ain't it?" he asked. "You wait here and I'll get my 'scooter.' I won't be gone a minute."

There was nothing incongruous to Victor about driving his bright-green motor bike out between hearse and limousine. He was back while Janice, still flushed with confusion, was looking at Sharon apologetically.

"I don't think Marie heard you," Sharon whispered. "She was talking to Russell. Marie would understand this, but she and her family are artists and wouldn't do it. All Italians love flowers."

"Who wants the first ride?" Victor asked, unmindful of the mourners who stood in subdued groups on the sidewalk. "I'll ride one of you around a couple of blocks, then catch up with the limping pedestrians and give someone else a lift."

They decided that Janice, as out-of-town guest, should have the first ride, so the gay green bike chugged quickly away with Janice on the little seat behind Victor.

"Who is this Victor?" Sharon asked Russell as soon as they were gone.

"He's a good guy," Russell assured them. "His uncle owns a lot of real estate around here and his dad works with him. Vic's got a job this summer as a deck hand on one of the excursion boats, and he's crazy about it. This is his day off or he wouldn't have been in the park."

"The excursion boat is probably a relief from his uncle's depressing business," Marie observed. "However, he has an imported motor bike and there isn't that kind of money working on excursion boats. He should think twice about a job with no future."

She sounded as practical and money-conscious as Janice. It was a side of Marie that Sharon had not seen before.

"The trouble is," she heard Russell saying, "he may not go back to school. He's seventeen and he should finish high school, but now that he's had a taste of earning his own money, and at something he likes. . . ." He left the sentence unfinished.

"His grammar could be improved," Sharon observed. "Otherwise he seems all right."

At Sullivan Street they turned back toward Washington Square, walking slowly and listening for the cheerful chug of the motor bike. Halfway down the block Sharon was startled to hear her own name called.

"Hi, Sharon! What're you doing here?"

Behind a high wire fence that separated the Sullivan Street Children's Center playground from the street was Jimmy, who had been tossing balls through a basket with two other boys.

Sharon stared. What was Jimmy doing at the Settlement playground? The Center certainly had more needy children than it could easily care for without Jimmy usurping its facilities and adding to the problems of the staff.

He came to the fence smiling. "They've really got the stuff here," he told his sister. "You should see the Circus Room. Ping-pong, chess, pool, everything! And the gym! Bars, basketball, pads for wrestling. Everything!"

"But what are you doing here?" Sharon demanded.

"I belong. You can join the Intermediates for twenty-five cents a year. It only costs ten cents if you're a Junior but I'm too old for that. Midgets only pay a nickle dues."

"But Jimmy, it's intended. . . ." She stopped, thinking of the boys who were listening. "When did you join? Does Daddy know?"

100

He disregarded her questions. "You should see the lunch they dish out for fifteen cents. Vegetable soup, salad, milk and chocolate pudding! Oh, boy! They got arts and crafts and everything!"

Sharon was still staring at her brother when Victor rode up and Janice jumped lightly from his bike, eyes shining and hair wind-tossed. Clearly she had enjoyed the ride.

"Hi, Jimmy!" she laughed and started toward the fence, then her eye caught the sign over the door of the adjoining dark-red brick building.

"Children's Center!" Janice's expression of pleasure changed. "Do you let Jimmy play at a *settlement* house?"

"These kids!" Sharon tried to laugh. Didn't Janice realize the other boys might be offended? Of course Jimmy shouldn't be here, though not because he was any better than the others, as Janice implied. He had a corner playground on his home street, a patio and parents. There were too many children who had no playground at all and who needed that lunch. But how was she to get him to leave all this equipment and fun? She looked toward Russell and Victor, wondering if either would have a suggestion.

Victor had taken in the situation with one knowing glance.

"How do you fellows like my scooter?" he asked the boys, who had stopped tossing balls. "Come on, Sharon. You're next."

He took her by the hand and almost pulled her across the sidewalk. "Come on, before they wise up," he whispered.

"What do you mean?" Sharon asked.

"Those kids ain't got any business on the playground on Sunday," Victor said, and pushed her gently onto the seat of

101

his bike. "It's never open without a supervisor on the job. I played there when I was a kid and I know the rules. Someone must have stolen the keys."

"Stolen?" The word choked her. "What are you going to do?"

"I'm going back to the park and get one of the cops before the kids wise up and beat it. If the cops get there first, there won't be trouble."

He had started the bike and she had to hang on. Did Victor really know that this was the thing to do? It seemed to her that she should be back there at the playground convincing Jimmy he should go home. How had he managed to elude both Mother and Daddy and get way over here without anyone knowing it? How was he to be kept out of mischief this summer if she didn't stay home and keep an eye on him constantly?

CHAPTER NINE

ERRANDS, UNINCORPORATED

IT WAS Sharon's first ride on an imported Italian motor bike, but she was conscious of only one thing: she was going with a boy she didn't know to get a police officer because her own brother had gotten onto the Settlement playground with stolen keys!

Sharon had scarcely seen the playground wading pool with its gay, hand-painted murals before Victor had hurried her past it. She'd had one fleeting glimpse of the vivid blue and green landscape on the walls—a remembrance of geese and dogs and children chasing butterflies. Then she was riding away down Sullivan Street. She didn't know whether Victor was driving fast or slow when he whizzed past the Legal Aid Society building and on to the Law Center of New York University, across the street from Washington Square Park.

SHARON

Resentment surged through her once more when the motor bike stopped at the corner for a traffic light. The clean, handsome red-brick university building, with its neat lawn and shrubbery, symbolized the reason why Jimmy was in trouble; why his continuous escapades threatened her own summer plans. If Daddy hadn't been forced to retire, she and Jimmy and the whole family would be vacationing now, far away from the hot city where there was nothing to do.

"Victor, please! He's my brother!" Sharon pleaded. "Have you got to get the cops? Can't you just go back and ask the boys to give you the keys?"

"They wouldn't do it. They'd beat it, keys and all. Nobody'd ever know who lifted them unless your brother told, and probably he wouldn't. The kids who play there regularly wouldn't tell."

"Jimmy doesn't know they're stolen!" Sharon was sure of it. "He'd never have talked to me the way he did if he had any idea anything was wrong."

"Then what are you in a stew about?" Victor asked, starting the bike again when the traffic light changed and spinning around to the entrance of the park. "We won't go back until after the cops have been there. Then we'll pick up the others. If it was my kid brother I'd keep out of it and see how he manages. It'll teach him something."

His eyes had been searching the park, and when he spied an officer he left Sharon.

Victor probably was right, she concluded. Jimmy did need a lesson. He wasn't taking responsibility the way Daddy and Mother had expected. He wasn't thinking of anything except sports and having fun. But the police! Sharon felt weak at the thought and waited miserably for Victor.

"What will the officer do?" she asked as soon as he returned.

"Give the kids a good lecture, take the keys, and send 'em on their way."

"They won't take them to the police station? Lock them up or anything like that?"

"Are you crazy?" Victor asked. "It's the cops who operate PALS for the kids. Organize sports for them and take them to ball games and stuff. They won't do anything unless one of 'em has a bad record. Violated a parole or something like that."

Sharon steadied herself against the motor bike at the suggestion of such a possibility and watched the broad blue back of the officer who had started down Sullivan Street.

"I guess I'll go home," she said. "As soon as I know he's all right."

"Aren't you taking this kind of hard?" Victor asked and looked at her critically. He had a way of looking people straight in the face, head cocked on one side, and he was practically staring at her now as though he would like to know exactly what was in her mind. "Kids get into mischief every day," he told her. "Come on and we'll park nearer the scene of the crime and see what's happening."

He drove around a block and stopped on a side street near the playground just as the officer got there. Sharon saw Marie and Russell and Janice walking on toward Washington Square and realized with relief that no one but Victor had sensed that anything was wrong. It was an even greater relief to see the boys all come out of the playground together, and while Sharon couldn't hear anything, she did see them start on their separate ways.

"Maybe you could give Jimmy a ride home," Sharon suggested. "I wish he'd go now and tell the folks what happened, himself."

"I'd rather take you home, or somewhere," Victor told her frankly. "This isn't the first time I've noticed you. It's the first time you weren't with that Brad fellow, though."

His mentioning Brad's name made Sharon want to go home more than ever.

"It's nice of you to want to give me a ride and I'd enjoy it, but I couldn't leave Janice. She's my guest."

"Some other time, then?" He made no move to leave her. "I'll go pick Jimmy up if you'll say when."

Sharon thought. She was going to have to arrange some fun for Janice. A date with Dick or somebody. If she wanted to be included, Victor was nearer her age than Dick's friends out at the Academy; they were interested in girls Janice's age.

"Call me in the middle of the week and see if I've worked anything out for Janice," she suggested.

"Why not take her on one of our cruises? We go to Far Rockaway and up to Rye Beach. Sail right out of New York harbor just like the *Cristoforo Colombo*! Boy, would I like to sail on one of the big ones. Really go some place."

Going on an excursion was something Janice couldn't do in Milwaukee, and it wouldn't be expensive. Sharon again told Victor to call her in the middle of the week, after she'd made some plans for her guest.

"That was a promise. Don't forget," he said emphatically, then headed toward the playground.

By hurrying, Sharon caught up with Janice and Marie and Russell before they were lost in the crowded park.

"Then I really don't know what there is to do," she heard

106

Marie saying, and there was a note of annoyance in her voice.

"Just no cultural appreciation, I guess," Janice replied. Then, seeing Sharon, "Where's Victor?"

"Giving Jimmy a ride home."

"That's good," Janice observed. "Maybe we should go home, too."

Sharon looked at Marie questioningly. Marie was digging the toe of her ballet shoe into the grass and saying nothing.

"You did want to see the exhibit, didn't you?" Sharon asked. "Why don't you and Russell go?"

"You don't mind?"

"Of course not. See you next week."

Sharon and Janice watched Marie and Russell cross the park, and for a few moments neither spoke. Then Janice offered an explanation.

"Either she heard what I said about the floral monstrosities, or she didn't like what I said about the Settlement House, or maybe it's just that I'm not the arty type." Janice sounded apologetic. "I didn't mean to offend your friend, but I guess I did."

"Maybe she had that art exhibit on her mind all the time," Sharon said. "She can be stubborn, too."

"Well, let's go home," Janice proposed. "It's sweltering in this park. Maybe we can think of something for tomorrow afternoon that will be fun for Jimmy, too. I'm going to see the Phillipses sail at noon. Want to come to the bon voyage party?"

"I can't," Sharon answered. "Mondays I swim at the Y in the morning and have typing until three-thirty in the afternoon."

107

"You could skip once, couldn't you?" Janice asked. "You never can tell what will happen at a bon voyage party or whom you might meet. Ed has nice friends."

It had been a long time since Sharon had seen a luxury liner leave New York harbor, and she was sure there would be an extra-nice bon voyage party, with flowers and refreshments and much excitement.

"It isn't that I wouldn't love to," she said.

"Then why don't you? Typing's good to know, I guess, but is it so important to you? What do you expect to come of it?"

"I wish I knew," Sharon admitted. "If you don't go to college you have to learn some skill or trade or something."

Janice edged into the narrow strip of shade close to the buildings. "Aren't you going to college?" she asked in surprise. "With your father on the faculty I thought of course you were."

Sharon hadn't said anything to Janice about Colorado, and now she felt compelled to explain.

"I've had my troubles and disappointments too," she said. "I tried out for a scholarship at a school I wanted to go to more than anything, and I didn't get it. I don't think I was intended to be a teacher or a librarian anyway, and that's what the folks have in mind for me."

"I don't think typing's a royal road to anything," Janice observed. "You're more the athletic type. Active, not chained to a desk. You manage kids pretty well, though." She seemed thoughtful. "Marie's the artist, all right, and she should go to the Chicago Institute of Art. I'm the one with no ability, so I'll go to the bon voyage party and hope 'something good may come of that.' Sure you don't want to come?"

Sharon was sure. Miss Moore was expecting her tomorrow. This week they might decide whether to approach the Director about a production. Now she wanted to get home and see whether Jimmy had told the family what had happened.

Janice, still uncomfortable in her silk dress, went upstairs to change, and Sharon hurried to the patio, where Daddy was watering boxes and pots of white and purple petunias.

"I guess he told you," Sharon ventured and sat down on the steps near her father. "Where is he? Down in the rumpus room?"

"Yes. He'll hide out until dinner time at least," Daddy said.

"What are we going to do now?" Sharon asked.

"I'll call the Director of the Children's Center in the morning and see if it's all right for him to use the facilities," Daddy said. "It was fortunate that Victor sensed the real situation and brought him home."

"Did you like Victor?" Sharon asked. "He wants us all to go someplace. Janice, Marie, everybody."

Daddy wiped the perspiration from his forehead and looked at Sharon closely. "He seemed to have good sense," he observed. "Your mother talked to him more than I did. See what she thinks, if he really asks you for a date. We don't know him at all."

Sharon didn't know whether Jimmy was embarrassed over the Sunday misdemeanor or whether overcast skies kept him near home the next morning. He walked Jato for a long time, then brought the little dog home. When Sharon started for the Y, he was playing with a bulldog that belonged to a neighbor who had it out on a leash. Jimmy knew the big dog well and was astride the animal, scratching its head and stumbling along clumsily, not really putting his weight on the dog. The owner looked half-amused, half-annoyed. Sharon stopped at Pop's store and waited for them.

"Pop, what are we going to do with Jimmy this summer?" Sharon asked. "Honestly! What do kids do who stay in town all summer?"

Pop watched the approaching man, dog, and boy. He sold a paper and package of cigarettes to a customer, then turned to Jimmy.

"Hey, you Jimmy! How much money you got in your pocket?"

"None. Why?"

"What'd you rather have, two bits or nothin'?" Pop asked.

"Think I'm stupid or something? Low IQ? Two bits, of course."

"Then I'll tell you what. You go over to that pastry shop where the two ladies sell fancy pies and stuff, and tell 'em you'll deliver. Tell 'em I sent you."

"Aw, they'll think I'm nuts."

"Not if you tell 'em I sent you." Pop leaned over his counter to adjust a pile of papers. "They wuz tellin' me yesterday they often have customers who order stuff special, and then can't come for it and want it delivered. The customers would pay."

"Mornings?" Jimmy asked.

"More likely late afternoon," Pop admitted. "But here's another thing. Why don't you take that wire tote wagon over to the chain grocery and see if you can't pick up some quarters by taking groceries home for people. Women come out of there every hour in the day, loaded down with more stuff than they intended to buy. Too heavy for 'em to carry, too."

"Aw, go on," Jimmy said.

"Go on yourself!" Pop snapped back, and his ruddy face flushed a deeper hue. He fussed and shoved at his stock of gum and candy bars and glowered at Jimmy. "There's enough odd jobs around this neighborhood to keep you earning money all summer if you'd just rustle them up."

"Do you really think so?" Sharon asked.

"I know it," Pop assured her. "Take these dry cleaners. They don't have enough delivery business to need a boy regular, but they get calls every now and then."

Sharon turned to her brother. The bantering, skeptical look had disappeared. Jimmy was interested.

"What we need is to set up a clearing house for odd jobs," Sharon suggested. "Why couldn't you do it, Pop? You know that place where people pin up notices about rooms or apartments to rent, or about wanting to rent something? The man got a lot of extra business after he let people tack up those notices at his place."

It was Pop's turn to look skeptical.

"Honestly," Sharon insisted. "People write their own notices and take them over there and put them up. It's no trouble for him. Then they buy something."

"Could be," Pop conceded. "All a lot of things need is someone to start 'em."

"We could organize something like 'Errands, Incorporated.' Only I guess it would be 'Unincorporated,'" Sharon said. "Kids like Jimmy could come here to see who needs errands done. They're here half the time anyway."

111

"Who'd let the folks know? The stores, I mean. Or other people who have odd jobs they need done?"

"Jimmy and the boys who'd like to do the jobs," Sharon suggested. "I'd help. Maybe we could put a notice in *The Villager*."

"Well, we could try," Pop agreed. "I suppose I could get me a whistle and blow a blast every time a call comes in for a boy. I've got a telephone and I wouldn't mind taking a few phone calls. Business ain't so rushin'."

"Gee!" Jimmy whistled. "Wouldn't that be something!"

"Well, go over to the pastry shop, then," Pop admonished. "And before it starts to rain. Maybe you'd better get your slicker and boots. You oughta do good on rainy days. And you, Sharon, talk to your folks about it. I sure hate to see these kids gettin' into trouble every summer just because they ain't allowed to work. The law forbids steady jobs at regular pay and regular hours, but this would be different. There ain't any law against a kid doin' an errand if he wants to. And it's work these kids need, that's what."

Sharon's mind was busy with the new idea when she went to the Y. "Errands" could be the answer to her worries about Jimmy. She'd talk to Mother and Daddy as soon as she got home.

At the Y Miss Moore was watching anxiously when the girls came in. Sharon was sure something was wrong, and by the time all were in bathing suits she knew what it was. Liz wasn't there, and neither was one of the girls Miss Moore depended upon to make up the outer circle.

The hour of practice didn't go too well. Sharon worked with the two beginners. They had learned to float, but their over-arm stroke wasn't good and she didn't dare mention the

112

crawl. Unless they put in a lot more time practicing, they couldn't participate in the close formations.

"Meet me again?" Miss Moore asked quietly when Sharon stopped beside her at the end of the hour.

They met in the same sandwich shop, and both were gloomy as the drizzling day.

"Liz called me yesterday," Miss Moore said as soon as they sat down. "She had a chance to spend two weeks in the country. You can't blame her."

"Liz doesn't worry me as much as those beginners," Sharon said. "She can step back into place as soon as she returns and be okay. Those other two will never learn the crawl in one summer. That blonde particularly. Besides, she's too short." She was overweight too, but Sharon didn't mention that.

"They don't have to master the crawl," Miss Moore assured Sharon. "We don't have to use that stroke in circle formations. We'll just have the crawl routines for those who can do it."

She took a pencil from her purse and began sketching formations on the paper napkin. "I just keep wondering if we can depend on Liz."

Sharon had her doubts, too. "We'd have to make her promise."

"I hate awfully to give it up," Miss Moore went on, drawing little swimming figures on the napkin. "You may as well know the whole story. Madeline Perkins isn't coming back in the fall. She's getting married, so there's a full-time job open and I want it! They'll have other applicants, of course, and people with more experience. All I ever did was help Miss Perkins last year, but I learned a lot. If I got the job,

I'd ask for you as assistant. If you'd like to work here part time, that is."

"Oh, Miss Moore! Would I like it!" Sharon could scarcely believe what she was hearing. "Let's go on with the Aquacade. When Liz comes back I'll make her *promise!* Then couldn't you ask the Director to watch us and see what she thinks?"

"That's what I'd intended to do," Miss Moore said. "We'd have to get approval."

Miss Moore's dark eyes weren't sparkling. She looked quite unhappy.

"You said we'd have to work two or three weeks before we said anything," Sharon reminded her. "It'll be three weeks when Liz gets back."

"It's risky, Sharon," Miss Moore warned. "We haven't a girl for replacement if one drops out."

"But let's not give up unless we have to," Sharon urged. "Just think how much fun it would be if you were swimming instructor and I the assistant. I can't imagine anything I'd like better."

"That's what I am thinking about," Miss Moore said. "You wouldn't earn a great deal, but it would put you in line. As for me, I don't know what I'll do if I don't get that job. I have to work. I must have a job next year."

CHAPTER TEN

BOAT TRIP TO FAR ROCKAWAY

In the middle of the week Dick Mendendahl called. Sharon hadn't heard his friendly voice in a long time, and his kidding was reassuring. She stretched out on the floor in the hall for a good long visit. If she could have had an older brother, Dick was the one she would have chosen.

"How expensive is this other cousin of yours?" he finally asked. "I'd like to meet her all right, and I'd sure like to do something in return for all the Sunday dinners Aunt Ardith has given me these last four years. But how expensive is quote Expensive?"

"I don't think it'll be too bad," Sharon told him. "We met a boy through Marie—you remember Marie?"

"How could I forget?" He assumed a tone of admiration. "I know. How could you fellows forget Marie! Well, as I was saying, this boy suggested the boat trip to Far Rock-

115

away, and it costs less than two dollars round trip. Janice seemed to think it would be fun."

"I guess I could finance that," Dick said, dropping the mocking tone. "It could be Saturday, couldn't it? I have to be back on the grounds at four on Sundays, you know. I've got plenty of boning to do between now and the finals, too."

"Saturday's all right. I'm not sure when the boat gets back, but we'll have our dinner here at home," Sharon promised. "Lunch at the beach shouldn't be too much."

He agreed to be at the Heaths' early, and, after special messages for each one in the family, said good-by.

"What are you going to do next?" Mother called from the living room, where she was busy with household chores.

"Call Marie and see if she'll come. She and Janice didn't take to each other particularly last Sunday, but I hope she'll come. Then I'll get in touch with Victor and see if he can get Saturday off. I don't know about his days off."

"That means four extra for dinner Saturday night, not counting Janice," Mother said, and for the first time Sharon thought of the work involved in preparing dinner for eleven people. Then there was the expense. She had always invited her friends home for meals since Mother had encouraged her to do so, but should she now?

"Oh, Mother! I shouldn't have. . . ." She looked from her mother to the telephone in her hands. "I haven't called Marie yet. Or Victor."

"That's all right. Go ahead and call them," Mother reassured her. "You can help me make potato salad Friday night. We'll manage."

"They're my guests, and I should pay for the dinner,"

Sharon said and put the telephone on the floor beside her. "What about the rent money Aunt Agnes was going to pay? You said I could have it. If she's sent it, you can use that."

"She sent a check, but Daddy hasn't agreed we should accept it," Mother explained. "We've never charged for our hospitality before. Don't worry about Saturday night. Call Marie and your other friend and invite them."

Sharon looked at the telephone for a few minutes without replying. "Maybe I'll have a part-time job in the fall, Mother," she began. "If Daddy'll let me have the rent for sharing my room, maybe I won't have to ask for allowance money any more."

"A part-time job?" Mother set the watering pot on the TV set and looked at Sharon in surprise. "What do you mean?"

"It's at the Y," Sharon explained. "It's not sure yet, but if Miss Moore gets the job as swimming instructor, she's going to recommend me as assistant."

"When would she need you? After school? Evenings?"

"I don't know, but I suppose so. That's when the girls come for swimming."

For a few minutes Mother considered the possibility, then she asked an unexpected question.

"Sharon, has Janice been talking to you about not going back to school?"

"Not about my not going," Sharon said truthfully. Did Mother and Aunt Agnes suspect that Janice wasn't going back to the University of Wisconsin? Sharon almost held her breath waiting for the next question, but Mother didn't speak right away. "I don't think Janice is interested much in what I do," Sharon finally added.

"We certainly haven't seen much of her," Mother mused. "I thought after her friends sailed she'd be with us more, but yesterday and today she said she was going shopping and to see some shows. I suppose that's what she came to New York to do."

Sharon knew her mother was looking at her and there was a question in her voice, but what could she say without breaking that promise to Janice?

"I honestly don't know what she's been doing since the Phillipses sailed," Sharon said. "I guess I've been thinking of myself. I really want that job, Mother."

"A part-time job at the Y would help with school expenses," Mother admitted. "But if you don't get it, we have the money for N.Y.U. all safe in the bank."

Sharon didn't reply. Both Mother and Daddy knew well enough how she felt, and Janice hadn't shaped her thinking. She still hadn't seen the guidance counselor about careers that weren't based on a college degree, but she certainly was going to do it before the summer was over.

"Go ahead and make your plans for Saturday," she heard Mother saying. "And help Miss Moore all you can. We'll see how everything turns out."

Things didn't seem to be working out too well Friday when Sharon arrived at the locker room. Scarcely half the class was on hand. She checked the girls off mentally as they darted out of showers and dressing rooms. Liz wasn't there, of course, nor two of the other "old-timers," and one of the beginners was sneezing and coughing. Sharon doubted that Miss Moore would let her swim that day.

They trooped to the pool together, one cough starting a

wave of coughing. The smile of greeting faded from Miss Moore's face.

"Don't tell me you all have summer colds!"

"I think just Lucille," Sharon said. "But two of the girls aren't here." She avoided looking at Miss Moore. No one except herself knew of Miss Moore's ambitious plan, so absentees didn't matter to the others.

Miss Moore shook her head. "No swimming for Lucille," she said. "Better go home and get started on your orange juice so you can swim Monday. The rest of us will begin."

Lucille didn't want to go home, but Miss Moore was firm. Practice started on the over-arm close formation, the girls swimming in twos across the pool, reversing without churning the water, and swimming back. Then, to the surprise of everyone, the missing girls appeared. There had been a traffic tie-up, they explained. Sharon and Miss Moore exchanged glances of relief.

"We'll try going into the circle with the breast stroke," Miss Moore called. "Sharon, take your position and I'll fill in for Lucille. Perhaps I can hold the formation at the other side where Liz should be." She put a waltz on the record player, gave a few more instructions and dived into the pool. With her skill and perfect sense of timing and direction, the circle took shape without Liz.

Sharon floated easily. The white tile ceiling seemed to be drifting rather than the girls in the pool. She was wondering whether it would be possible to work with Lucille sometime next week. What the girl needed was more practice. And about two more inches in height and ten pounds less weight, she thought wryly. Monday she'd find out about Lucille—

119

where she lived and what added time she might give to swimming. This Aquacade couldn't be given up now when it almost surely meant jobs for Miss Moore and herself.

The ceiling drifted by, and the seats beside the pool. Sharon saw them as they were last May, filled with gay, applauding spectators. Her parents had been there and Brad and Debby's father, who had arranged to have part of it filmed for showing on his TV show later that evening. It had all been so wonderful . . . dancing on the roof with Brad, seeing their own performance on TV. . . .

So absorbed was Sharon with the memory that she didn't grasp the full significance of what she saw while room and pool were floating by. She was conscious of the figure of a woman standing in the entrance way, quietly observing. Just a trim lady in a dark blue dress, almost out of sight. Then she recognized the Director!

Sharon caught her breath sharply. Her arm muscles tightened, one knee came up with a jerk, and she was out of position. The girls whose hands touched hers lost their positions too and the circle was broken.

"All right, girls! You did pretty well." Miss Moore looked at Sharon but saved her question for their regular "shop talk" at the restaurant.

Sharon was there first and held a booth in the corner until Miss Moore came. She was too worried to look at the menu and began talking before Miss Moore had settled herself on the opposite bench.

"I couldn't help it," Sharon began. "Do you know who was watching us today? The Director!"

"What?" Miss Moore's brown eyes were round with surprise. "Are you sure?"

"I saw her. That's why I practically submerged and ruined everything. I was so surprised! Honestly, I could just die."

"Well, don't," Miss Moore advised. "I wish she could have dropped by when we had a full class, but anyway we had a formation. Now I've got to see her, though. I can't wait."

"Liz'll be back a week from Monday. If I could coach Lucille sometime between now and then . . . then if the Director would watch us a week from Monday. . . ."

Miss Moore reached over and squeezed Sharon's hand. "I'll talk to her as soon as I can get an appointment. We may as well know what she thinks right away. She's sure to have figured out what I've been scheming."

"You'll let me know what she says? You'll call me? I don't think I can stand the suspense until next week."

"If I see her before then I'll call you," Miss Moore promised. "Now let's see what they have for lunch. How about a bowl of chili and a glass of milk?"

Sharon took a paper napkin from the container and rubbed at the black table top. "I'm not hungry," she said.

"You've got to keep your strength up, girl," Miss Moore said in her usual cheerful voice. "This was a surprise, not a calamity. What about chili? It's good here. Not too hot."

Sharon felt better after she'd eaten lunch. Miss Moore didn't think the Director's visit had been too great a misadventure; perhaps everything would be all right.

Miss Moore called her that evening, and her first words were reassuring.

"Sometimes everything works out for the best," the instructor said, and laughed her contagious laugh. "She's going to look in on practice a week from Monday. Your suggestion,

121

dear, remember? Now if Liz will return on schedule, I think we'll get the green light."

"Wonderful!" Sharon almost sang the word. "She didn't think we were out of line for trying without asking her first?"

"She didn't seem to. How could we tell whether we had a question to ask, if we didn't try out first?" Miss Moore's reasoning sounded logical. "Now, did you really mean what you said about giving Lucille some extra help?"

"Of course I meant it."

"Then here's her telephone number. Take it down and see what you can arrange. She really does need help."

Sharon called the number right away but no one answered, nor could she reach Lucille on Friday. She'd have to wait until the girls came back to the Y on Monday.

Saturday was a clear, warm day and the Heaths had just started breakfast when the doorbell announced Dick's arrival. Jato and Jimmy fell over each other in racing to the door, and at the unusual commotion, Peeky began his chant: "Where-you-been?"

Dick came into the dining room slowly, his dark-blue, visored cap in one hand, the other extended to Mother, and he smiled at each member of the family in turn. Dick was large-boned and built like Daddy, but he was shorter and somewhat stocky. His hair was auburn, his hazel eyes arched by heavy eyebrows, much darker than his hair. Sharon noticed Janice taking him in with one quick look that saw everything but seemed so casual. He wasn't handsome, Sharon realized now. She liked him so much that she scarcely thought about his looks.

"Janice, this is our nephew, Dick Mendendahl," Mother

said. "We've all had fun with Dick these past four years."

That the whole family admired and approved of Dick was evident. Nancy and Cathy had left their places at the table to vie for the honor of taking his cap. Janice extended her hand and smiled her most charming smile. Yes, she would like Dick too, Sharon was sure. In his navy-blue Merchant Marine uniform, immaculate and with brass buttons shining, he certainly looked like an "able seaman," as they had so often joked.

Janice had prepared for this meeting, also. She was wearing a new white sun-back sport dress and it could not have been more becoming or fitted her better.

"How about hot blueberry muffins and a cup of coffee?" Daddy offered, inviting Dick to the table. "What time do they have breakfast out on Long Island? Daybreak, I suppose."

"Long before that," Dick said as seriously as though it were true. He drew up the chair Daddy indicated and took the coffee and muffins Mother offered.

"How many are going on this cruise?" he asked. "Sharon? Jimmy?"

"Not me! Jimmy announced. "I've got a really big job today. All day, maybe."

"A job?" It was a chorus.

"The Major over at Evangeline Residence bought some second-hand furniture for the roof garden and when it came it was a mess, so I've got the job of cleaning it. This 'Errands Unincorporated' idea of yours is okay, Sharon."

"Errands" had to be explained, so Sharon told them how Pop and she had tried to figure it out.

123

"Maybe I'd better go talk to Pop about it seriously," Daddy suggested. "Now that I think of it. . . ." He looked at Jimmy and left the sentence unfinished. Jimmy hadn't been in mischief all week.

"Who's the 'Major,' and what's 'Evangeline Residence'?" Dick asked Jimmy, giving the boy his full attention.

"Evangeline's a great big residence house for girls who work," Jimmy explained. "Secretaries and stuff. It's big as a hotel and the Major is the boss. He wears a blue uniform something like yours. Only it's the Salvation Army uniform, not the Merchant Marines."

Sharon remembered the Evangeline vaguely and it brought to mind the Y.W.C.A. residence in the Village, Spelman Hall. If Janice should carry out her idea, there were places she could live besides the Heaths'. Sharon couldn't think about it now, though, for it was time to start for the Battery, where Victor and Marie and Marie's date would be waiting for them.

It developed that Marie had invited her tutor, Hal Newman. Victor gave the slim, studious-appearing young man one look, then started plying Dick with questions, practically forgetting the girls. He was wearing his own navy-blue outfit and he straightened his shoulders perceptibly and walked with a new snap when he fell into step with Dick and started across the park for the boat tickets. When they rejoined the girls, who had waited on benches near the excursion docks, it was obvious that the conversation had been entirely about the Academy.

"What does it take to get in?" Sharon heard Victor asking. "I mean, who do you have to know? My uncle's got a

124

pull with our Congressman. He's an undertaker and pays a lot of taxes."

"It's not who you know," Dick told him. "It's your high school grades and record. You have to pass an examination and write an essay. It isn't as hard to get into as Annapolis or West Point, though."

"Does knowing anything about boats help?" Victor pressed. "When we go aboard I'll show you the engines."

Janice turned from the two seamen to Hal. "I hope you're not nautical," she said, and smiled winningly. Then with Hal at her side they all followed Dick and Victor through the crowd to the boat.

It was a large, white excursion vessel with two upper decks, and its whistle was calling the passengers. Early arrivals left the benches or patches of shade where they had been feeding pigeons. Latecomers began running from the ticket window, for the excursion boats left promptly on schedule. There were family groups with children, tourists with cameras and "See New York" guides, older people with books and magazines, and many teen-agers with bathing togs. Janice had a bright candy-striped bag, obviously new, and quite in contrast to the battered blue one Sharon carried in her hand.

"This looks like it's going to be just dandy for you and me," Marie observed aside to Sharon, giving Janice's back a disgusted look.

"Dick won't let it go too far," Sharon assured her. "See?" He was turning around while she spoke, waiting to cross the gangplank with the girls. Just as they came up to him, however, a boy of about thirteen or fourteen moved a wheel chair through the crowd into position beside them. A woman with a young face and short-cut silver hair was seated in the chair. One foot was in a cast. With her hands she was trying to help elevate the wheels to the gangplank, and her hands fascinated Sharon. They were large, with long fingers, and she wore huge rings with identical mountings on either hand, one stone an amethyst, the other jade. She was wearing a pale orchid-colored suit.

Dick was instantly at the boy's side. "Can I help you, fellow? Here, let me give you a lift."

His strong arms raised the wheels easily and the chair moved across the gangplank without a jolt. The woman thanked him gratefully, her dark brown eyes shining and her face alert and eager.

"Better put her over here," Victor directed. "The shade'll be on this side when we turn around. Unless you want to get the sun?" He was giving her his full attention now. She was really stunning looking.

"We can move the chair easily, once it's on level ground," the woman said. "It's just getting off and on that's difficult."

"I'll come back when we dock," Dick promised. "Don't worry."

"That would be very kind of you." She looked from one couple to the other. "It won't be too much trouble?"

"We'll be back," Victor assured her. "Now we're going to look at the engines."

Once more he started away, leaving the girls to their own devices. Dick hesitated.

"I'm sure you girls can get along without us for a few minutes," he said. "How about going up where it'll be cooler?"

126

"I guess we can stand the coffee and hot dog atmosphere a little while," Marie told him. "We might get separated if we went to one of the upper decks. There's quite a mob aboard."

"Oh, I think they could find us," Janice objected. "Come on, Hal, everybody."

It was Hal's turn to hesitate, but Janice was starting toward the stairs. "Do you mind if we go up?" she asked Marie.

"Not one bit," Marie almost snapped. "In fact, I think it's a very pleasant plan!" Then she turned her back on Janice and Hal and walked over to their new acquaintance, who had been quietly observing them. "I hope your foot isn't hurt too badly?" she inquired.

Marie's acid tone had stopped Janice. Sharon waved her toward the upper deck. "I'll stay with Marie," she said quietly. "Go on up. We'll find you."

It was a bad way to start their outing, but it seemed best to wait with Marie, so she followed her friend to the woman in the wheel chair.

"I was beating my brains out typing a paper on the Archeozoic Era and didn't realize the typewriter was slipping off its stand," she heard the woman explaining. "It had just been cleaned and the man hadn't clamped it back on properly. So, crash-bang it went on my foot and broke a couple of bones. Foot bones are awfully slow to mend."

Both Sharon and Marie were sympathetic. "Are you able to get to your job some way?" Sharon asked. "I hope your employer is understanding about it, if you can't."

"Fortunately I'm my own boss," the woman said. "I'm a public stenographer and I have my own office." She extended a hand toward the boy, who was still standing beside the wheel chair. "David wheels me over every morning and back home at night. A friend drove us down to the Battery in his station wagon this morning and he'll pick us up when we get back. We thought we could manage the rest by ourselves. David's my big boy and he's really strong and resourceful."

Sharon smiled at the boy, who was eyeing the hot-dog stand, but she scarcely heard the last of his mother's explanation. It was the first two sentences that kept repeating themselves. Would she dare ask this spectacular-appearing woman about her work? How had she become her own boss? What did a public stenographer actually do? This was her chance to find out. Twice she opened her lips, then hesitated to voice her questions. Marie started to move away but Sharon held back. She must ask!

"I hope you won't think I'm rude or too inquisitive," she began. "I do want to ask what a public stenographer does, and how you got to be your own boss."

The woman smiled and gestured with one ring-laden hand. "Take a course in typing and shorthand, rent an office in some hotel where business men have offices or live permanently, and print some business cards. Easy! You charge more for your services than an ordinary stenographer gets, but you work when and as long as you please. And you beat your brains out for the money. Ask me. I know!"

She flipped at her short silver curls and the green jade ring picked up the summer sunlight. People were looking at her and she knew it. She opened a large white purse and gave Sharon her card. "Maureen Whiteman, Public Stenographer," Sharon read. Then the address caught her eye. Maureen Whiteman had her office in one of the large hotels at the edge of the Village, and the two telephone numbers were both Village exchanges.

"Why, you work and live in the Village!" Sharon exclaimed. "I live right off Waverly Place." The woman seemed much less formidable now. "How did you know about being a public stenographer? How do you get people to bring their business to you?" The questions poured out.

"My father often used public stenographers' services and that's how I knew," Mrs. Whiteman explained. "So when my husband died and I had to support David and myself, that seemed the best and quickest way. No long, expensive training course. Six months in a good business school."

Sharon realized she was staring, but she couldn't help looking at Mrs. Whiteman. "Could anybody do that?" she asked.

"Well, you're a bit young," Mrs. Whiteman said with a smile. "It helps to have contacts in the business world before you start." She looked at Sharon appraisingly. "You aren't through school yet, are you?"

"I'm through high school and I'm taking typing."

"Drop by when you're ready to start work," Mrs. Whiteman suggested. "There are times when I have straight typing jobs like manuscripts and reports and things. Stop in anyway." Then she smiled again, the flashing, friendly smile.

Sharon thanked her. "I will," she said. "And we'll see you when the boat docks."

She joined Marie, who had walked toward the stairs. New York harbor was slipping away from them, the wharves of Brooklyn on one side, Staten Island on the other. Already they had left Governor's Island and the Statue of Liberty behind, and were tooting and chugging their way past the tankers and towboats, ferries and small private craft in the Narrows, out toward the great Atlantic.

Sharon didn't see or hear the sights and sounds of the harbor. It didn't matter whether Victor paid any attention to her on this boat trip or not. She opened her faded beach bag slowly, found her old red leather wallet, and put Mrs. Whiteman's card away where it would be safe.

CHAPTER ELEVEN

SOMEONE IN JANICE'S CORNER

SHARON started toward the stairway leading to the upper deck, her mind on some day months ahead when she would have finished a course in typing. She could see herself going into the big hotel on lower Fifth Avenue, saying "mezzanine" to the elevator operator, and walking into Mrs. Whiteman's office. "I'm Sharon Heath. Do you remember me?" she would ask, and the dark eyes would light with recognition. "You told me to drop by when I finished my course and I finished yesterday." In her lovely daydream she had a certificate in her purse showing she had completed the work with high grades, and she was dressed fashionably like Mrs. Whiteman and Janice.

"For one who's practically been stood up you look very happy," Sharon heard Marie saying, and the words brought her back to reality. She looked at her friend quickly. Marie was tapping her fingers against the iron railing and frowning with annoyance.

"Oh! Dick and Victor. After the Diesel engines, we come next."

"After the Diesel engines and the gal from Milwaukee!" Marie was really angry, and Sharon hoped she would try to hide it when the group reassembled.

"It's just as much Hal's fault as hers," she said.

"The way I feel about him at this moment!" There wasn't any question about how Marie felt. "Only he's my tutor and he's got to get me through math or I can't get my high school diploma, so I've got to be nice."

"You are peeved, aren't you?" Sharon asked. "I never saw you so upset about a mere boy friend before."

"It isn't Hal, really," Marie told her. "It's that cousin of yours. Sunday she couldn't be bored with the Salmagundi Club or Frank's artcraft shop either. I offered to take her over and open it up, but she wasn't interested. You weren't among those present when I made the grand gesture and was spurned. Now she walks off with my date."

"I wish she hadn't, but she's nearer Hal's age than we are," Sharon reminded Marie. "And Frank's copper shop." She shook her head. "There isn't any lovelier hand-wrought jewelry anywhere. She doesn't realize. Not that it's any excuse."

"I'll never ask her again and that's final!" Marie told Sharon. "I probably wouldn't have been quite so . . . well, hurt, I guess . . . only Frank's wife had to go home to Italy last week. Her father sent for her because her mother's sick. If anything should happen and Frank had to go, I'd have to take over."

132

"Oh, no!"

"We can't afford to close the shop with the summer tourist business in full bloom," Marie went on. "I guess because she's one of them I expected her to be interested, and I guessed wrong."

For a few moments the girls stood side by side, watching the receding shore line and the small craft steaming in and out of the harbor.

"You can do the hard soldering now, can't you?" Sharon asked.

Marie nodded. "I can enamel pretty well, too, but I can't work in the window and take care of the customers too, and it's that action in the window that gets the crowds. Besides, when you put an enameled piece in the kiln it has to come out in exactly three minutes, not five or ten or half an hour later."

"Maybe Frank won't have to go," Sharon said, trying to be optimistic. She was wishing Marie and Janice had not taken such a dislike to each other. Janice could help Marie in the shop if Frank really had to go to Italy.

There was no time to think about the problem, for Dick and Victor came sauntering across the deck to join them.

"Where's everybody?" Victor asked with his usual directness.

"Everybody went thataway," Marie answered, indicating the deck above.

Victor didn't seem to notice the sarcasm in her voice, but Dick looked at Marie sharply. "Let's find them and close ranks," he suggested.

They found Janice and Hal on the upper deck staring silently at the blue-gray, shimmering ocean and the liners that looked like beetles against the haze of the far horizon. Janice made no move to relinquish Hal, even though they all remained together for the rest of the trip. So Dick did his best to entertain Marie and Sharon listened with half her mind while Victor talked endlessly about boats and his experiences on one trip after another.

Sharon was the first to suggest going below when the sliver of land that was Far Rockaway appeared. She led the way, her eyes turning to the place by the rail where they had left her new friend, Mrs. Whiteman. The wheel chair was not there. For a moment Sharon stopped, looking over the crowd that was gathering near the gangplank, then realized she could not stand on the narrow staircase in the way of other passengers.

But where was Mrs. Whiteman? Dick was looking for her too, and it was he who spied the white hair and orchid-colored suit first.

"I guess she's found some other people," he said, indicating the crowd pressing against the ropes. There in the front ranks was the brown oak chair, and a man with a boy about David's age was holding it firmly.

Sharon could scarcely hide her disappointment, even when Mrs. Whiteman turned to look over the crowd behind her. Dick waved and when Mrs. Whiteman saw him she smiled, but it was a good-by smile. Sharon would have to go to the office on Fifth Avenue if she ever saw Mrs. Whiteman again.

She was still wondering how a public stenographer got the contacts Mrs. Whiteman had said were necessary while she walked from the boat to the bathhouse and changed into her plain blue bathing suit. She knew Janice had bought a new suit, since she had not brought one from home, and Sharon wondered what it would be like. When she saw her cousin she realized once more how well Janice knew color and line. Her suit was a brilliant carnation pink. Marie, in a copper shade slightly darker than her skin, was equally attractive. Sharon hadn't bought a new suit this year and in her last season's faded blue, her only compensation was the knowledge that she could swim and they could not. Even their helplessness was appealing, however. Victor and Hal were willing instructors.

For the first time that day Sharon was alone with Dick. They swam briskly for a time, surface diving and twisting, until they were tired and sought the shade of the pavilion and a cool drink.

"Now bring me up to date," Dick said, settling down beside her. Elbows on the table, his firm chin in his hands, he looked at her seriously. "Where's Brad? And who is this Victor?" He wasn't smiling and his eyes were asking for honest answers.

"I thought I told you Brad's gone up to the Cape," Sharon began. "He's been waiting to hear definitely when you graduate so he can invite the old crowd up for a week to help you celebrate. Victor's a boy one of Marie's friends knows, and I didn't have anyone else to invite."

"Okay," Dick said. "I just wondered."

"For Victor, boats are all there is, I guess," Sharon went on. "He's trying to make a good impression on you."

Dick nodded. "He wants to come out to the Academy and see the place, but I didn't know whether to mention graduation exercises or not. He could really get an idea of the spirit of it then, but I wasn't sure about you and your folks, and whether you'd want him along."

"It's all right. You can invite him to come with us. Mother and Dad and everybody will be coming."

"That's another thing." Dick was still sober and unsmiling. "What about your father?"

Sharon pushed her drink aside. "Honestly, Dick, I'm so worried. He hasn't any job after summer school is over. He keeps going to agencies and having interviews, but nothing comes of it."

"It's only a month since the University closed, isn't it?" Dick asked.

"Yes, but he didn't wait until the end of the school year to start looking," Sharon explained. "He and Professor Burns were talking all last year about retirement and 'Past Sixty' Clubs and things like that."

Dick moved the paper cup across the table. "Two of the men out at Kings Point are retiring this year," he said thoughtfully. "The chaplain and my physics instructor."

"What are they going to do?"

"The chaplain's going out West to help his son, who's in some business or other. I don't know about Captain Culver," Dick admitted. "I heard some rumor that he's going abroad. He's missed classes more than once this spring. I wonder if he's been having trouble too."

"Interviews, probably," Sharon said, and the bitterness she felt sounded in her voice. "Interviews that don't amount to anything and just beat him down. I suppose Captain Culver's taught all his life, too."

A frown clouded Dick's face. "This isn't like you," he remonstrated. "A man has to do what he's fitted for and enjoys doing. Victor'll never be satisfied unless he goes to sea, and I feel the same way about it. Captain Culver and your father were meant to teach. They've been examples to more young people like us than you'll ever realize, I guess."

There was rebuke in Dick's voice, and Sharon didn't answer.

"What needs to be done is to change this system that forces a man to retire when he's able and willing to work," he went on. "Something for our generation to do, maybe. In the meantime, I'd like to have your Dad meet Captain Culver when you come out for graduation. Now tell me about this Janice. Why is everyone down on her?"

"Down on her?" Sharon repeated in surprise.

"Am I wrong?" Dick asked. "With Marie, it's out in the open. Aunt Ardith wore a worried look every time she glanced in her direction this morning, and you practically put a hex on her by labeling her 'expensive.' Give a look over there."

"Over there," at the opposite end of the pavilion, Janice was eating a hot dog and a plate of French-fried potatoes and laughing with Hal. In her vivid pink bathing suit she made a pretty, happy picture.

Sharon felt guilty. Glancing at Dick, she found the hazel eyes looking at her unflinchingly. "What's the score on Janice?" he pressed.

In the four years since Dick had come to New York, four years in which Mother and Daddy had taken him into the Heath household as though he were a son, Sharon had never kept a secret from Dick. Now it was impossible to tell him Janice's story. She had promised not to tell. She had kept it from her mother. How could she tell him? Sharon shook her head and looked toward the white sands of Far Rockaway Beach, the hundreds of sun bathers moving up and down, or stretched on blankets, or jumping in the waves.

"Maybe what Janice needs is someone in her corner," Dick suggested. "I'm going to ask her for another date."

Nothing Dick could have said would have been more surprising. As a favor to Sharon he had agreed to escort Janice on this outing, and Janice had turned away from him to spend her time with Hal. Yet now Dick was going to ask her for another date. Did he feel that Sharon had been at fault because Janice had not gotten on well with the Heaths or their friends? Sharon had expected Dick to be on her side always. She had been sure he would understand that Janice had been a problem and that he would share her disappointment over the scholarship too. Now she didn't want to talk about the one or the other. She wouldn't even mention the decision she must make before the summer was over.

Sharon drew a long breath and got up. "I guess I'll go hunt for the post card stand," she said. "Maybe I'll mail some cards."

Dick got up with her. "Let's both send cards to Brad," he suggested.

"Brad and Debby and everybody," Sharon said, trying not to show how she felt. With all her heart she was wishing for her old friends. Janice had done nothing but cause trouble for everyone. Was she going to alienate Dick, too?

CHAPTER TWELVE

A LITTLE SHOP IN THE VILLAGE

Sharon didn't know whether Dick asked Janice for a date or not, but before the evening was over Victor was proposing one thing after another to do for fun. Summers in New York City were not new to him.

"What about square dancing up in Central Park?" he asked while they walked to the neighborhood movie that evening.

"That should be gay," Sharon said.

"Then there's Palisades Park and Coney Island, only Coney's too crowded. You can't see the water for the people."

"There'll be concerts in Washington Square Park, too," Sharon said, recalling the announcements in *The Villager*.

"What time does Dick have to be back on week nights? How long is Janice going to stay? Or would he take Marie if we went dancing? I like to dance, don't you?" Victor was eager and a little breathless.

"You can ask the questions all right, but I don't know the answers to any but the last one. Yes, I like to dance."

"Then you and I can go, only I thought it would be fun to have Dick along," Victor told her. "We can go up to Rye Beach or to Keensburg swimming, too. You're really the mermaid. I was watching. Don't think I didn't notice who could swim."

Sharon was sure he had noticed. Victor's dark eyes, constantly on the move, would see everything. He was looking at her intently now and he moved closer to her side and took her hand. Ahead of them Dick and Janice were talking together quietly but they weren't holding hands, and Victor observed that too. Self-consciously he gave Sharon's hand a quick squeeze then dropped it and once more squared his shoulders and started walking with Dick's sure step.

Victor deferred to Dick in everything. After the movie he waited while Dick decided where they should go for a Coke.

"It isn't just girls who are impressed by a uniform," Sharon said aside to Marie while the boys were talking.

Marie was still disgruntled. "You have to admire Victor for recognizing that Dick has something worth while," she said. "Something Victor probably wants, too. He may have played up to Dick, but he hasn't ignored you."

"I know you haven't had much fun today," Sharon sympathized. "If we do any of the things Victor suggested, you'd better invite a boy your own age and not someone Janice would be interested in. All we can do now is forget it."

As for Sharon, she soon forgot it. Too many other things began happening the next week. Monday morning at swimming class Miss Moore told the girls about the Aquacade.

"You didn't know it, but you've been practicing for something special," she began. "It's about settled that we're going to have a water show at the end of summer. You're that good."

"What?"

"We are?"

The pool resounded with noisy exclamations and questions.

"You can invite your parents and boy friends and anyone you want." The instructor extended her arms in an all-inclusive gesture. "We'll put a row of chairs along the viewing side of the pool and if we're as successful as last spring, the standing room will be taken too. Pretty good, us! Yes?"

"No!" It was Lucille, and instantly everyone was looking at her. In her dark-blue bathing suit, sitting on the side of the pool and kicking at the water with toes that barely reached it, she was a picture of gloom.

"What's the matter?" Miss Moore asked. Some of the animation left her face, although she still sounded cheerful.

"The rest of you may be that good, but I'm not. I can't swim in any public performance."

"You're learning and you're doing all right," Miss Moore assured her. "Sharon's offered to put in extra time teaching you the easier strokes. You don't have to do the dives or crawl or anything tough."

Lucille shook her head. "I haven't any extra time," she insisted. "Nor any money for the extra pool fee."

The girls began talking in little groups of two or three, or jumped into the pool.

"If it's just the pool fee, forget it," Miss Moore began. "You could get the time, couldn't you?"

141

Lucille shook her head again. "I can't. Besides, that isn't it! You know I can't swim."

"You can float," Sharon reminded her.

Lucille pulled her bathing cap off, letting her long brown hair fall to her shoulders. Wasn't she even going to stay for class practice? Sharon wondered. Then the girl turned to Sharon almost angrily.

"How would you like to be the only one in a water show who couldn't swim?" she demanded. "And I know how I look in a bathing suit as well as you do. I know I'm too short . . . and I bulge!"

"You can't help being short, of course," Miss Moore admitted. "But you can join one of the gym classes—'Maid to Measure' or 'Posture and Poise'—and it would improve you a lot. You certainly can help by not spoiling this affair for all the other girls. You don't have to take part in any of the ballet formations or routines except the one we've been practicing."

Lucille's sulky expression changed slowly. "I don't want to spoil it for the others, but I don't want to look like a dope in front of a lot of people, either."

"Maybe you're better than you think," Miss Moore said, and her smile and tone were encouraging. "Let Sharon concentrate on you today while I go through the routines with the rest of the class."

The instructor walked to the diving board and blew her whistle. "Surface dive, everybody! Go into it slowly . . . slowly . . . stiff from the hips down. Don't stay under more than three minutes!"

She was laughing again and the girls laughed with her. Reluctantly Lucille reached for her cap, and Sharon held back a sigh of relief. If she could just keep Lucille coming to the pool and teach her to hold position, Miss Moore would work out the program all right.

"You can master the over-arm easy," she assured her pupil. "The crawl's harder because of the breathing, but the over-arm's a good stroke."

Lucille looked dubious.

"You and I could do a formation together," Sharon went on. "I'd stay with you and swim at your speed and keep you on a straight line."

"You think we could?"

"Lie on your side," Sharon instructed. "Your right hand is just a paddle, or a fin or something. Now up and over with your left hand and pull for power, see? Cut the water with your legs like a shears."

Sharon demonstrated, and held Lucille at the midriff while she tried. She didn't cooperate wholeheartedly, however, and Sharon felt she would do no more than take her place in the one formation, if she did that much to help with the Aquacade.

It was hard not to worry about Lucille during typing, and it was all Sharon thought about on the way home. Turning the corner from Waverly Place, she was surprised to see Nancy and Cathy in front of Pop's stand, each with a popsicle, and Nancy clutching at Jato's leash. Where was Jimmy? Sharon hurried the half block to the stand, but before she asked the question she saw her father inside talking to Pop. He motioned her to a stool beside him.

"What would you like?" he asked. "Pop and I are talking about 'Errands.'"

Sharon ordered a Coke. "Where's Jimmy?" she asked.

143

"Delivering prescriptions for the druggist around the corner," Daddy answered. " 'Errands' will be a going concern yet. Pop's willing to act as a clearing house, but we need to get the word around. I thought I'd try my hand at writing an announcement tonight. How good are you as a typist?"

"Oh, Daddy! Not that good!"

"You aren't?" He sounded disappointed.

Sharon started to say she really wasn't, but the memory of Lucille and the Aquacade came back to her. Getting this project operating would keep Jimmy occupied and off her mind while she finished her summer program. It would help a lot of other neighborhood youngsters too. Typing the announcements would take time and it would be hot down in Daddy's den, but she knew she would do it.

"I'm afraid I'll make mistakes," Sharon apologized. "We can't erase in typing class. I suppose I could erase on these."

"And why not?" Pop asked. "Just so they can be read, that's all."

"I'll keep the announcement short," Daddy promised. "Then as fast as Sharon can get copies typed, Jimmy can take them around to the shops. I can talk to some of the store-keepers myself and explain the idea. I think the plan is really important. We've had no trouble with Jimmy since 'Errands' got under way."

Sharon knew it was true. She hadn't even worried about him for days. She watched while Daddy pulled an old envelope from his pocket and began listing neighborhood stores.

"Oh, before I forget it, Sharon, there's a letter at home for you, and Marie called this afternoon," Daddy said. "She wanted you to come to the copper shop as soon as you can."

Sharon was sure the letter must be from Brad. She

144

went home first and found it on the table in the hall. Eagerly she tore the envelope open.

"Dear Sharon (and I don't mean the boat):" it began. The sight of his handwriting made her lonely and the letter made her lonelier. Brad and his family had sailed down to Martha's Vineyard, where they'd picked up Debby and some new friends she had made. They'd been around Nantucket Island and up to Marblehead. It all sounded so wonderful. But Brad had missed her and there was comfort in his last paragraph.

I can hardly wait for Dick's graduation and 'Our Week.' I've played *The Sharon's* theme song so many times that Mom's hidden the record. They sure aren't painting the skies so bright this year!

"Wish you were here,"
Brad

Sharon read it twice, then tucked it into her purse and started for the copper shop. She tried to tell herself that sailing to Far Rockaway with Victor had been fun too, but it wasn't the same. Victor wasn't Brad!

It was only a few blocks to the neighborhood where narrow Fourth Street wound its meandering way through the Village. The window shoppers moved slowly along the hot pavement from one display to the next, admiring the handwrought silver, the leather goods, paintings, and piles of wicker baskets in shop windows, some overflowing onto the street. Sharon darted around the leisurely groups, bumping into a woman who was having her feet measured for sandals on the sidewalk in front of a leather shop.

Sharon saw Marie as soon as she approached Frank's store, for she was in the window soldering clasps onto the

145

backs of a pair of earrings. People on the sidewalk were watching her, and two young girls were leaning over the counter that separated her workbench from the store, observing every move.

"Won't Ruth be amazed when we tell her," Sharon heard one of them saying when she entered.

"It'll mean so much more to her, knowing we saw them made."

The blue flame from Marie's small soldering iron flickered and flared and sputtered gently until she shut off the gas. She pushed the small metal tank aside and turned for a gift box.

"We make every piece," Marie told the customers. "We buy flat eighteen- or twenty-gauge copper sheets and cut the pieces with hand shears. Everything except the backings for earrings and pins is made right here."

She gestured toward the workbench, cluttered with hammers and jeweler's saws, rules and calipers and jars of oil and powdered glass. She smiled while she made change, but the moment the customers were gone she dropped into the chair beside the bench with a groan.

"Sharon, won't you save my life and run around the corner to the delicatessen and get me a sandwich?" she begged. "I've been working all day without a bite."

"Frank . . . ?" Sharon knew what had happened without asking.

"He left this morning. Flew to Rome. I should have known better than to come to the shop without bringing a sandwich, but I was so upset I forgot."

Marie wiped her damp forehead and reached under the counter for her purse and compact. "I haven't even had time to freshen up," she apologized. "This shop is all one person can handle, believe me."

"I'll get you a Hero with salami and cheese and tomatoes and everything," Sharon promised and hurried out. When she returned Marie had the counter covered with pins and bracelets and earrings and was trying to help a stout, fastidiously dressed woman decide upon a gift while other customers waited. Sharon stepped behind the counter to help. One person couldn't manage the shop alone.

"What are you going to do?" she asked Marie when they closed the door for the day. "You'd better come home with me now. You don't want to eat dinner alone tonight."

"I sure don't," Marie said with a grateful sigh. "Gee, how I wish you weren't tied up at the Y every day."

Sharon thought of Janice, doubtfully. Perhaps when Marie explained what had happened Janice would offer to help. If she only knew how lovely the shop was, with handsome necklaces and pins hanging everywhere and the work so interesting to watch.

The idea occurred to Mother, too, when Marie told her story at the Heath's dinner table that night. While plates were being filled Mother turned to Janice.

"I know you came to New York for a vacation," she began. "Would experience in one of the best-known shops in the Village be something you'd like to remember?"

Everyone was looking at Janice, and Sharon heard Marie catch her breath at the suggestion she had not expected. Janice set her fork down on her plate and closed her hands tightly at the edge of the table.

"Oh, no!" Marie spoke up quickly. "I didn't mean for you to do anything about it, Mrs. Heath. I already know how Janice feels. Everyone can't be interested in arts and crafts, I guess. No, I wouldn't want Janice to give up her vacation."

Janice bit her lip, her cheeks flushed, and for a moment she didn't speak.

"It isn't that I wouldn't like to help," she began. "Only I don't see how I can. I'll have to be leaving pretty soon. You've put up with me long enough. I'm going to call Mother in a few days. There're some people I want to see. . . ."

"That's all right, you don't have to explain." Marie sounded relieved that Janice had not responded to Mother's suggestion. "Don't worry about me."

"You don't mind if we do, though?" Daddy asked, and reaching over he patted Marie's hand reassuringly. "Sharon, don't you imagine typing those notices for Pop and Jimmy would be almost as good practice as you'd get in class? You could put in an hour or two early each morning, typing them here at home, and then go to the shop and help Marie."

Sharon felt as though she had known all along who would help Marie. Hoping that Janice would offer had been wishful thinking.

"Could I get away long enough Friday morning for swimming?" she asked Marie. "And again Monday, if Frank isn't back by then?"

"I don't want you to miss your classes. I'll get along," Marie said, but she was looking at Daddy gratefully. "Swimming's only a couple of hours, portal to portal, isn't it?"

"When are you going to call Milwaukee, Janice?" Mother asked, changing the subject. "I'd like to talk to Aunt Agnes, too."

The worried look Dick had mentioned was obvious to

Sharon now. The food on Mother's plate had scarcely been touched.

Janice picked up her salad fork and avoided Mother's eyes. "I'll let you know," she answered evasively. "I don't want to call her if there's nothing important to say. There're some things I wanted to find out first . . . get settled first. . . ."

Sharon glanced at her cousin. Janice was staring at her untouched salad and her chin had a stubborn set.

CHAPTER THIRTEEN

"ALL THE GIRLS GO TO NIGHT SCHOOL"

SHARON was glad that Mother suggested she stay all night with Marie, since Janice and Marie and she never would have managed an agreeable evening together. Janice offered to take Nancy and Cathy up to the playground as soon as dinner was over, and Marie and Sharon strolled back to the little court known as The Mews where Marie lived.

"Have you ever told Janice our place was once a carriage house?" Marie asked. "If she knew the studio houses on this old cobble-paved lane originally were stables for the millionaires. . . ."

They turned into a narrow private street where no automobile traffic was allowed. Sharon surveyed the little houses, each with prim old-fashioned shutters, a tiny bit of boxed shrubbery at the door, or vines climbing over brightly painted façades. Swank new apartment hotels towered above them on the streets surrounding The Mews, but Sharon had always preferred the Togliotti's studio apartment, which they had inherited from an artist friend when he moved to Mexico City. To her, there was an air of gentility about each of these special streets in the Village—Washington Mews, MacDougal Alley, and even Minetta Lane—which kept alive the memory of Minetta Brook, the turbulent stream that once crossed Washington Square. Daddy had said there was nothing to the story that the brook still babbles in a subterranean cavern beneath the park, but Sharon loved the legend and she never went into Holley Hotel without stopping for a moment before the exquisite fountain the Village Historical Society had erected there in memory of the brook that had been diverted, years ago, in the name of "progress."

"The way Janice is, well, maybe it's my fault," Sharon said. Janice certainly hadn't caught the spirit of the Village, where streets followed the old cow paths of New Amsterdam and past and present lived side by side. "If I'd started out taking her around to the places we like it might have been different. But she started with the Phillipses—headquarters at the Plaza. Now I don't know what to do. She's got such different ideas."

"I'll say she has," Marie agreed. "What has she been doing these past three weeks? We've seen her about twice."

Sharon thought she knew what Janice had been doing, but all she could mention was shopping and shows.

Sharon and Marie and Daddy had agreed that Sharon would spend two hours each morning typing the notices about "Errands." If she began at eight o'clock she would be free to help Marie soon after ten, and few customers came in before that hour. Sharon hurried home the next morning to start her task and found Daddy still reading the paper.

"I've bought a new typewriter ribbon," he said when she leaned over to kiss him. "We'll move the typewriter out of the den into the rumpus room and turn on the fan. You won't be too uncomfortable. If you get the notices all typed in two or three days, maybe you can find out what your class is doing and practice the same work at home."

She followed him downstairs to his den. The newspapers and magazines he had been saving for so long were piled on two old tables, and when Daddy switched on the light he stopped to look at them, a puzzled expression on his face. Finally he began to smile, then laughed loudly.

"Look at this, Sharon," he said, and pointed to the headlines on one of the papers. "Babe Ruth Hits. . . ." He turned to the next one. Inch-high headlines proclaimed Carl Hubbell as "King."

"Jimmy's been having a wonderful time for himself while we thought he was doing penance," Daddy laughed. "Oh, my!"

"No wonder Pop didn't know where he got all his information!" Sharon looked at the piles of papers Jimmy had stacked neatly against the wall, each one opened at the sports page.

Daddy continued to chuckle while he set up the typewriter stand for Sharon. "Your 'Errands' idea will keep him and the rest of the boys occupied, I hope," he said. "Ready to get started now?"

The first page went slowly. Halfway through it Sharon made a mistake and left out a sentence. After that she copied more carefully, word for word and line for line. She had three notices finished by ten o'clock and was tired of sitting in one position. She gave the pages to Daddy and hurried to Fourth Street.

Marie was spreading oil on small copper ovals, preparing them for the colored powdered glass and the enameling kiln, but it was not her work that flushed Marie's cheeks.

"Sharon, what do you think! Maybe I know what Janice has been up to," she said as soon as Sharon entered the shop.

"What? What do you mean?" Sharon asked.

"Who do you suppose just walked into the side door of that snazzy French restaurant across the street on the corner? Janice!"

"No! Why would she go there? Even for a cup of coffee?"

" 'Cup of coffee!' " Marie scoffed. "At ten o'clock in the morning? They don't serve breakfast there and she couldn't be meeting anyone, because the place doesn't open until about eleven."

Sharon leaned on the counter and looked up the street at the big restaurant, with its heavy satin draperies drawn at the windows. Janice had said she was going to get a modeling job, but perhaps Marie's guess was correct. A customer came in while she was still looking and she had to get out articles and quote prices, but her mind was still on Janice. As soon as the woman left, she turned to Marie.

"I've got to find out if what you think is true. If it is, she's got to tell Mother," Sharon said. "This can't go on. She made me promise not to tell certain things, but this is different. I'm going to find out before the lunch crowd comes in."

Marie dropped a small piece of copper wire onto her enameled base, turning it deftly with the tweezers.

"I guess you'd better," she agreed. "It's probably legal for her to work there. She's nineteen, isn't she? But your mother should know."

Sharon left the copper shop with scarcely a thought about how she looked or what she would encounter. The restaurant wasn't the kind of place where schoolgirls in white cotton blouses and red skirts dropped in, she realized, but her appearance wasn't important now. It was what she would say to Janice if her cousin actually had a job and was working there.

Heat and sunlight from the street streamed into the dimly lit, air-conditioned dining room when Sharon opened the door. Immediately in front of her were tables glistening with shining silver and glassware, and farther down the room men in black coats and white aprons were setting up other tables. Janice was standing before a counter placing single roses in bud vases, and with a forced smile of welcome she reached for one of the large menu cards that lay in a pile beside the cash register. Her smile changed to a startled "Oh!" when she saw Sharon, and she turned to look back into the long room with its rows of white-covered tables.

"Janice! So you have a job. You're working and you haven't kept your promise!"

"I don't know whether I'm working or not," Janice answered under her breath. "How did you find out? How did you know?"

"Marie saw you. Frank's shop is right in the next block, only you didn't know that. You weren't interested," Sharon said accusingly. "And this isn't what you told me you were going to do, and you haven't told Mother or . . ."

"Wait," Janice interrupted. "I'm not sure I have the job.

The man said he'd try me out for a few days. Please, Sharon, don't say anything yet."

"But you said you were going to get a job modeling," Sharon protested. "There might be a career at that, I don't know. There certainly isn't any future here."

Again Janice interrupted. "I can't get a job modeling. Not fashions, anyway. You have to be five feet four and I'm just five feet two. I've seen every agency in New York, I guess, and they all told me the same thing. But I met a girl at one of the places and she said she got her start here, as a hostess. She said a lot of commercial artists and advertising men come here." Once more she looked apprehensively toward the back of the room.

"Janice, you're always telling me not to be 'ridic.' I think this is 'ridic,'" Sharon said. "And you've got to tell Mother or I will."

"Not yet," Janice begged. "If they give me the job I'll get a room somewhere. I know you're tired of sharing your room and I don't blame you."

"It isn't that," Sharon said. "If you had a job that would amount to anything, and were getting a room at Spelman Hall or Evangeline Residence, our folks might not object. But this! Just a chance that someone will notice you and offer you a job. Just a chance for glitter! You can't expect me to keep it from Mother now."

"Wait," Janice repeated. "How do you get a room at Spelman Hall? Mother would know the Y is all right. Maybe if I had a room there it would be all right."

Sharon hesitated. "Will you come up to Central with me the first thing in the morning?" she asked. "If you'll talk to the guidance counselor about everything, I won't tell tonight.

But I mean *everything*. Modeling and this hostess job and the room and everything."

A door at the back of the room opened and a large man in a black suit started slowly along the aisle, surveying the tables.

"Go, please," Janice urged. "That's the boss and you've kept me from getting the vases on the tables."

Sharon didn't move. "What about tomorrow morning?" she demanded.

"I'll go with you if you won't tell," Janice said, while she fumbled to disengage a rose from the pile of flowers on the counter. "Now scram, please!"

Outside the restaurant, in the heat and sunlight, Sharon wondered if she had done the right thing in almost threatening Janice and in agreeing to keep her secret for one day more. One day probably wouldn't make any difference. She'd call the guidance counselor for an appointment as soon as she got back to Marie's store. She would have to tell Marie something, but Marie wouldn't talk if Sharon asked her not to.

All summer Sharon had been thinking about visiting the guidance counselor. The personal service office was in the same building as the swimming pool and the club rooms. She wondered during that busy afternoon, and again in the morning when she and Janice started out together, what the counselor would be like, and whether both she and Janice could talk to her at the same time.

Neither girl had much to say on the bus ride, and Janice nervously twisted the handles of her purse more than once. Sharon was uneasy, too. Suppose she was questioned about her own plans? She didn't know what she was going to do next fall, or in the years ahead. She had promised herself she would talk to Mrs. Whiteman as well as the counselor, but she had been afraid to talk to either of them. Afraid the counselor would say that of course she should go to college; afraid Mrs. Whiteman wouldn't think her six weeks of typing instruction qualified her for even a beginner's job. By the time she reached the Central Y she was as nervous as Janice.

A young Chinese girl at a desk outside the counselor's office greeted them and asked which one was Janice Ross. The girl was dressed in a blue cotton print not unlike the hot-weather dresses Sharon and Janice were wearing. Her hair was cut short and she wore the summer sandals all the girls had that season.

"Mrs. Knight is expecting you," she said to Janice and, motioning Sharon to a chair, led the way to an office down the hall.

There was nothing to do but watch them go, and with them the chance that Sharon could talk to the counselor today. In a way it was a relief. Sharon watched the receptionist come back, walking with a slow, easy step. She picked up a book from her desk that appeared to be an economics textbook, then put it aside for a moment and looked at Sharon.

"Would you like something to read?" She motioned to magazines on a table near her desk.

"Perhaps, if it's likely to be a long interview," Sharon answered.

"It could be," the girl told her. "Mrs. Knight hasn't made another appointment for an hour."

An hour. Sharon sighed. "Do you work here? All the time, I mean?" she asked.

"Half days," the girl replied. "I go to City College in the

afternoon and another girl takes this desk. We just see each other at noon when we say 'Hi' and 'Good-by.' "

She didn't exactly smile. Her round face was placid and unemotional, but her lips curved gently and there was a friendly light in her dark eyes. "You won't mind if I go on studying?"

"Of course not. Don't mind me."

Sharon picked up a magazine but she couldn't read. It was disturbing to think other people were working out sensible plans for a future—that probably Janice would come out of that inner office with something tangible to do, while she still had only a vague idea about working and no plan for her future at all.

When Janice did return her eyes were red and her handkerchief crumpled. Mrs. Knight, a plump and middle-aged lady, came with her and walked directly to Sharon.

"I should know you," Mrs. Knight said. "Janice tells me you belong to the Y-Teens and swim here in our Aquacades." She smiled, disregarding Janice's forlorn appearance.

Sharon said yes. What could have happened in the counselor's office?

"Why don't you two girls go down to Spelman Hall and look at the house and the rooms?" Mrs. Knight suggested. "Then Janice can decide whether she wants to ask her mother about living there. If you'd like to do that, I'll call the director and tell her you're coming. It may be easier to decide after you've seen the place, Janice."

Sharon didn't know what to say. This wasn't what she had expected. Was Mrs. Knight saying Janice would have to ask her mother before she could have a room at Spelman Hall? Sharon had expected the counselor to settle every-

159

thing—where Janice could live and what she should do. She felt embarrassed to look at her cousin, but unexpectedly Janice stepped closer to her.

"Would you have time to go with me?" she asked.

It was the first time that Janice had ever looked forlorn or in any way inadequate. It was the first time she had ever asked anything of Sharon. Clearly Janice's plans weren't settled and she did need a friend "in her corner," as Dick had said.

"Of course I'll go with you," Sharon told her. "We'll call Marie and then go."

Janice managed a smile at last and turned to say good-by to Mrs. Knight.

"I'll do what you said about the Bell Laboratories," she said.

"Then good-by for now, and let me know what your mother says." Mrs. Knight smiled. "Good-by, Sharon."

Sharon led the way to the powder room without being asked. Janice's eyes and nose did need attention, and she looked at Sharon gratefully when she sat down before the mirror. Sharon sat on the bench beside her, watching thoughtfully. She wanted to ask what had happened in the counselor's office but it seemed too personal.

"What are the Bell Laboratories?" Sharon asked at last.

"Bell Telephone Company," Janice explained. "Mrs. Knight said several girls who've lived at Spelman Hall got jobs there. They teach you how to do something when you don't know anything, like me. One year in college certainly doesn't prepare you to earn a living."

"No, I guess you need the works," Sharon agreed.

160

"Mrs. Knight said there are things you can learn to do on the job and the Bell Laboratories train you. They have clerical jobs and filing jobs and running the mimeograph machines. They have some system for up-grading, too."

It didn't sound much like the glamorous modeling job Janice had come to New York to get. Sharon remembered that first night when Janice had tossed the rhinestone bracelet onto the bed and defiantly declared she wouldn't go back to Milwaukee. Apparently she still felt that way. The memory seemed to come back to Janice too.

"She didn't think modeling was impossible, but you have to train for that too," Janice went on. "Artists use models for hats and jewelry and stuff. It isn't all clothes. But she said John Robert Powers himself didn't recommend it as a career. You're out of work more weeks than you work. Powers wanted his daughter to teach school, she said."

"Teach school?" Sharon repeated.

"Maybe you'd better think about it some more," Janice advised. "Ready now?"

Spelman Hall, the Y.W.C.A. residence, was in the Village, a large brick building that looked like an old-fashioned hotel. It faced another little triangular park like the one at the end of Sharon's street. The lobby was large and airy and more like a living room than the entrance hall of a hotel or institution. The grandfather's clock had a friendly tick, prints on the walls were splashes of bright red and green and yellow, divans and chairs were large and inviting. Opening from the lobby was a parlor with furniture in gay summer slip covers, a grand piano, books and magazines.

Mrs. Knight had phoned the Director and she came in a

few minutes, greeting both girls cheerfully. She was a small woman, not much bigger than Janice, with a quick step and eyes sparkling with enthusiasm.

"I'll be with you in a minute," she said. "Let me drop these papers on my desk. Here's the bulletin board. Take a look at the notices and you'll have an idea of what the girls do who live at Spelman Hall."

The bulletin board was filled with announcements. Inexpensive jaunts like hosteling through the Berkshires, a boat trip to Bear Mountain, a bus trip to the Pennsylvania Dutch country. There were notices of evening courses the various universities were to offer in the fall, notices of church festivals, requests for volunteers at children's day camps. There were even business cards from employment agencies.

When the Director took the girls to the elevator, they found the walls covered with more notices—the time for rehearsals of various groups, personal things for sale or exchange, and cartoons apropos of jobs and dating.

"It looks like 'never a dull moment,'" Janice observed when the elevator started.

"Would you believe it, these girls are so busy with night school and part-time jobs and rehearsals for shows and parties here at Spelman, that we finally had to give up serving the evening meal," the Director said. "We couldn't find any hour when they could all get back for dinner. We only serve breakfast now. Here we are. I'll show you a single room that's vacant. Mrs. Knight said you were going to write your mother and if she agrees to your plan, you probably could have this room. It looks right out on Abingdon Square."

It was the smallest bedroom Sharon had ever seen. The walls were pink, the bedspread and draperies blue, the dresser, desk, chair and single bed all diminuitive. She glanced at Janice and knew exactly what her cousin was thinking. So did the Director.

"You won't be in this room except when you're asleep," she told Janice. "You'll be in the game room or the television room or rehearsing with whatever group you're interested in. What are you studying?"

"I'm not studying anything," Janice told her. "I'm going to apply for a job at the Bell Laboratories. This afternoon."

"You'll be studying something before a month is over," the Director predicted. "They all are. Dancing, singing, acting, languages, jewelry making. I never saw anything like the girls who come here to live. If they don't have an interest when they come they soon acquire one. It's contagious."

It was what Janice needed, Sharon thought when they returned to the long, clean gray halls and the bright orange doors. Through one open door she glimpsed another room, walls covered with college pennants and a collection of flower prints. On the floor two young, dark-skinned girls were stretched out studying. Both were dressed in play suits such as Sharon often wore, but they looked foreign.

"Those are two scholarship students from Liberia," the Director explained when they were all in the elevator and the door closed. "We have some exceedingly brilliant young people. We had five foreign girls on scholarships last year."

Back on the main floor she led the way to a plaque on the wall. "Before you go I'd like you to know about the house," she said. "It was built more than fifty years ago as an inn. Trowmart Inn, it was called. In 1920 it was presented to the Y.W.C.A. as a memorial to Laura Spelman Rockefeller by her husband, John D. Rockefeller."

Side by side, Janice and Sharon read the inscription.

"I'm sure you'd like the girls if you came here to live," the Director went on. "They do have fun. Look around as much as you like. You'll find the date parlor and the TV room this way. There's a laundry room and a sewing room." She pointed the way.

"Do you really need your mother's permission to live here?" Sharon asked when they were alone. "I didn't know that."

"It's the way they want it," Janice explained. "Mrs. Knight made me feel I wasn't being fair with Mother, and they have to consider parents' feelings, too. Maybe she won't object when I tell her about this. And I'm going to the Bell Laboratories right away. Then I'll go over to the library tonight and walk home with Aunt Ardith and tell her."

They turned from the plaque to the bulletin board again. The notices were fascinating.

"Look, Sharon! The Camera Club is going on a 'bird shoot' next weekend. Do you suppose if I called Mother instead of writing, and if she would ship my camera equipment right away, do you suppose I could go too?"

The elevator door opened with a metallic clang and three girls in shorts, each carrying a tennis racket, bounced out laughing. An older woman with a dog on a leash had come into the lobby to talk to the woman at the reception desk, and her pet licked one girl's bare leg. With screams of laughter all three raced out of the house. Janice turned from the notice of the Camera Club hike to watch them, eyes shining with anticipation.

"Maybe we'd better get started," Sharon suggested. "You

ought to call the man at the café and tell him you're not coming back. I've got to help Marie, too."

Somehow she felt let down. Was she the only one in the world who didn't have things under control? The only one who just knew what she did *not* want to do?

CHAPTER FOURTEEN

PLANNING COMMITTEE

THE telephone was ringing that evening when Sharon came home from the shop. It was Victor calling her. She settled down on the floor, her back against the wall seat.

"I tried to forget you but I couldn't," he said with mock mournfulness. "What are you doing Friday night besides going with me to the square dance up in Central Park?"

"I was thinking of a trip to the Pyramids or the moon or something," Sharon laughed.

"Shall we do that before we go square dancing or after?" He sounded very sure of his date with her, she thought.

"Who is going square dancing?" she asked.

"Us. You and me and Dick and Janice," he told her.

Sharon was surprised. Janice hadn't said anything to her about a date with Dick. "When did you and Dick schedule all this?" she asked.

"Just now. He's going to call Janice tonight. I was just talking to him."

"I must say you two are quite sure of yourselves," Sharon said. "Suppose Janice and I had other plans?"

"Well, if it's just dates with other boys you could call them off, couldn't you? For us, couldn't you?" He was trying to be humorous but he didn't sound quite so self-confident as at first.

"We might consider it," Sharon agreed. "We'd have to give it serious thought, though."

"Unless you get too serious, I'll be at your house at eight-thirty Friday night. Okay?"

"I'll have to ask Mother and I don't know about Janice's plans. Give me an hour and call me back," Sharon told him.

"Will do. Gladly. It's an awful long time until Friday night. I hate to think of how long. But if I can call you, that will be a big help."

"Flatterer."

It was nice to hear him say it, just the same, and nice to have something pleasant to do. For a few moments after she hung up Sharon sat on the floor thinking about Victor . . . how he looked, and his quick, direct way of talking. She didn't remember ever knowing a boy who was so uninhibited and so eager to be doing things.

She thought of Brad, too. Going with Victor wasn't being disloyal. Brad and she hadn't even talked of going steady, but actually that was what they had been doing throughout her senior year in high school. He hadn't asked her not to have dates with other boys this summer either, and he'd gone to Martha's Vineyard to visit Debby. He'd taken Debby and her family on a cruise around the Cape and up to Boston and back.

Sharon was still sitting on the floor, the telephone on her knee, when Mother and Janice came in. They were holding hands, and when Sharon looked questioningly at her mother, there was no anxiety in the answering smile.

"You run along, Janice," Mother said. "Sharon can help with dinner. If you send the letter air mail tonight, Agnes may get it tomorrow."

"Aunt Ardith thinks I should write it all out and ask Mother to call me after she's read the letter," Janice explained to Sharon. "And I got a job. I can start Monday morning in the duplicating department if she'll send me my birth certificate so I can prove my age . . . and if she'll let me stay, of course."

"You got a job? So soon?" Sharon asked in surprise. "Are you lucky! I wish I could do something like that."

"Like what?" Mother asked, and stopped on her way to the kitchen.

"Get a job and stay out of school a year," Sharon said. "I can't see any sense in going to college if you don't know what to take. It didn't do Janice any good to go to college for a year, just taking liberal arts."

"What were you going to take if you went to Colorado?" Mother asked. The question silenced Sharon, and she was glad when the clanging telephone interrupted the conversation, for a truthful answer would have been "liberal arts."

"Guess who?" a girl's voice giggled when Sharon said hello.

"Debby!" Sharon exclaimed. "Debby, where are you? Not here? In New York?"

"In person. Coming to you 'live.'"

169

"How come?" It was good to hear Debby's voice again. Sharon had forgotten how offended she had been the last time she saw Debby.

"It got so boring up at Martha's Vineyard. Nothing to do but loaf," Debby told her. "Then Daddy has to put his show back on, and we've got to buy my clothes for college, so we came down for a couple of days. A bunch of us."

"A bunch?" Sharon asked.

"Well, two or three people," Debby admitted. "And look. I called the program director. The Y-Teen Planning Committee can meet Friday afternoon, now that I'm back in town. We called everybody. We always hold one meeting in August, so it'll be Friday if you can come."

It was good to be talking about Y-Teen plans. Sharon knew the four officers and the seven other committee chairmen who made up the Planning Committee. It would be fun to see them again.

"What time?" Sharon asked. "Make it as early in the afternoon as you can. I'll be there for swimming in the morning anyway, and I have to get back and help Marie in the shop as soon as I can." Then she told Debby about the trouble in Marie's family, and finally they agreed to meet at one-thirty.

"Maybe there'll be another surprise for you," Debby said mysteriously after settling the hour for meeting.

"What?" Sharon asked. She knew she had been holding the telephone line for a long time again, but what could Debby mean?

"I'm not telling," Debby held out. "It wouldn't be a surprise. See you Friday."

The Program Planning Committee and the possible surprise were exciting to think about until Friday finally came. First there was swimming and her work with Lucille, who was struggling with the over-arm stroke and making slow progress at best. Then lunch with Miss Moore and a wait on the club floor until the Planning Committee assembled in the big meeting room with its long conference table and rows of chairs along the wall.

Debby, as president, was there first. She was browned from days in the sun, her hair had been cut very short, and she was wearing dark glasses with elaborate green rims and bows, ornately decorated with rhinestones. Her dress, however, was a plain, harmonizing shade of green and she had eliminated all jewelry. She was being sophisticated again, but she seemed sincerely glad to see the committee members.

There was Johnny Tate, the Negro boy who was vice president; Sari Tazmanian and Audrey Jacobs, secretary and treasurer respectively, and the various committee chairmen. They came from all parts of the city. Some were children of well-to-do parents and others worked to pay their Y dues, but they had common interests and worked together harmoniously.

Debby called the meeting to order promptly. She was quiet and businesslike and seemed to have gained poise since the last meeting before school closed in the spring.

"Audrey, let's have your report as representative at the Summer Conference," she began. "With two hundred girls there, from Connecticut and New Jersey as well as New York, you must have picked up some ideas we could incorporate into our program next year. Or at least consider."

Slender, studious Audrey gave a serious report. A girl

171

from the Hong Kong Y-Teens had been a guest at the Summer Conference, and while it was difficult to bring back more than a glimpse of activities in a Chinese Y-Teen Club, Audrey did have a concrete suggestion.

"She was just as interested in our activities as we were in hers," she told the committee. "I'd like to see one of the Interest Groups in our Y-Teens get up a scrapbook with lots of pictures that would give Y-Teens in some other part of the world a true idea of New York City and how we live and what we do in the different Interest Groups. Our holiday parties and dancing and singing and club work. All of the Interest Groups should take part, each one furnishing snapshots and clippings from newspapers about its own activities. Then next spring we could send the scrapbook to Hong Kong."

They voted at once to recommend that activity for next year's program. Craft groups, dance groups, discussion and social relationship groups, and above all *Y-Quill News* were to combine their efforts and produce the scrapbook.

"Why couldn't the *Y-Quill* write up the project early in the fall?" Sharon suggested. "The *Quill* goes all around the world. Other clubs might take up the idea and make scrapbooks too. We'd have clubs in Bombay and Calcutta exchanging with Brazil and Sweden. Who knows how it might spread?"

"A chain reaction," somebody suggested.

Other program ideas were offered eagerly. There wasn't any lack of enthusiasm for carrying them out, and more than once Debby had to rap for order and get the discussion back to the matter of the program itself.

Sharon felt a glow of satisfaction when the meeting came to an end. There were activities to link all the Interest

172

Groups in several special projects, and she had been made responsible for the vocational guidance sessions.

While she waited for the others to say good-by to Debby, an idea suddenly came to her and she edged into the crowd, impatiently trying to extricate her friend.

"Look," she said in an excited undertone. "How long are you going to stay in town?"

"Just over Sunday."

"Couldn't you stay longer? Or come back, maybe? Gee, Debby, you could save the summer Aquacade if you'd come back. Miss Moore's trying so hard to make it good, and I've floundered around coaching a new girl who can't swim. If you'd stay, Liz would take the beginner's place and you could come back into your old spot. Oh, Debby, if you only knew!"

"Knew what?"

"How much it means. It may make the difference between Miss Moore getting a full-time job as swimming instructor, or not. It might . . . well, that's it!" She couldn't bring herself to tell Debby of her own hope for the job of assistant.

"Miss Moore's really okay, isn't she?" Debby was wavering. "Is it going to be open house again?"

"Just like last spring when your Dad had it televised," Sharon assured her. "Remember Parents' Night, when the girls danced with the fathers and the boys with the mothers?"

Debby remembered. "I'll have to see what Mom says about two trips back to the city," she said. "I'd like to help Miss Moore. Who wouldn't?"

It was a hope, and Sharon clung to it. She felt good about the whole afternoon, and on her way home she thought about the vocational guidance program, wondering how she could

173

make it better than last year's. It was then that she came to a decision about visiting Mrs. Whiteman. She would really do it, and now.

Visiting Mrs. Whiteman started out the way Sharon had imagined it. She knew the big hotel, and the elevator operator let her off at the mezzanine floor without looking at her. To the far left she saw the sign "Public Stenographer." She felt choked and nervous when she walked down the hall, and at the open door she stopped, for the voices that came to her were loud and angry. Mrs. Whiteman, trim in a black silk suit, was standing in the center of a small room that was equipped only with two typewriter desks and chairs and two filing cabinets.

"I quoted my prices when you left the work," she said to a stout, middle-aged man who also was standing. He had a large manila envelope in his hand and a slip of white paper which Sharon decided must be Mrs. Whiteman's bill.

"You quoted me a price per page and now you bill me a price per hour," he said, shaking the white paper. His face was flushed and he was frowning.

Mrs. Whiteman glanced from her customer to Sharon and gave her a quick nod of recognition.

"I quoted both rates," she insisted. "This was a very difficult job—a technical paper badly written in longhand. I did the work myself, and I had to stop and look up terms three or four times on every page. It was an awful job and you know it."

"What was so awful about it? A few technical terms. I supposed an expert stenographer was acquainted with basic English."

"'Basic English!'" Mrs. Whiteman scoffed at the words.

174

"I'm not going to argue. The paper was filled with technical words and the writing was terrible. That's my price."

"All I'm going to pay is the per page rate you quoted." The man slapped the large envelope down on the desk and drew a billfold from his pocket. Before he could take the money out, however, Mrs. Whiteman took the envelope and extracted a manuscript, leaving the typewritten pages.

"Here's your copy," she said, and her dark eyes were flashing with anger. She turned to her metal filing case and with a quick gesture put the typed pages inside and closed the door with a bang.

Sharon held her breath. The amazed man stared at his penciled sheets speechlessly.

"The transaction's over," Mrs. Whiteman said. "Sorry we didn't please you." Then she turned to Sharon. "Come on in, honey. I remember you."

Sharon hesitated before going into the office. The man was still standing there, red-faced and furious. He looked at the bill again, counted out the money and put it on the desk without a word. Mrs. Whiteman delivered the typed manuscript and her disgruntled customer left without even replying to her "good-by."

"Sorry you walked in on a scene," Mrs. Whiteman said and drew a long breath. "We don't have them very often, thank heavens. Sit down. How are you?"

"I'm fine, but I guess I came at the wrong time." Sharon was sure of it.

"Well, it's over. You're the girl who was asking about being a public stenographer, aren't you? On the trip to Far Rockaway?" She had recovered her composure and was smiling. "What's on your mind?"

175

"You said sometimes you had extra typing," Sharon began. "I'll finish my typing course in two weeks, but I don't know. I'm sure I couldn't do anything like that," and she glanced at the open door.

"All the work isn't difficult," Mrs. Whiteman told her. "I'd have to try you out, of course. How old are you?"

"Sixteen."

Mrs. Whiteman shook her head. "You'd have to get working papers. You know that?"

Sharon had heard girls at school talk about working papers, but she didn't know what was involved in getting them.

"I'll have extra typing from time to time after college starts in the fall," she heard Mrs. Whiteman saying. "You finish your course. It wouldn't be fair to try you out until you're through. Then I'll see how many words you can do per minute on straight typing. What did you plan to do? Just work after school?"

Sharon shook her head. She hoped to have a job at the Y for after school—a job which certainly seemed more pleasant than this.

"What I was really thinking about was staying out of school next year," she began. "I don't know what I want to do and I thought I wouldn't start college until I did know."

Mrs. Whiteman tapped her typewriter with bright red fingernails. "This would be rather uncertain," she said. "It's a feast or a famine. Sometimes I don't have enough work to pay the rent, and the next week I have more than I can do, sitting up all night. I couldn't promise anything definite or regular. But if you want to come back after you've finished the course I'll try you out."

Sharon knew the interview was over. The prospect for a job with Mrs. Whiteman wasn't very good, and the job would be much less desirable than she had imagined. Uncertain income, disgruntled customers, long hours one week and no work the next. It wasn't what she had expected.

"Good-by, honey. Come and see me any time." Mrs. Whiteman's hands, with their massive rings, were already reaching for papers on her desk.

"Good-by, and thank you," Sharon said. She was too subdued to say she would come again. She was sure she wouldn't, in fact. All she had learned from her interview was one more thing she didn't want to do.

CHAPTER FIFTEEN

KINGS POINT

UNDER a circle of double floodlights the huge cement skating rink in Central Park shone invitingly. Dancers, and those who had come to watch, were filling the surrounding seats when Sharon and Janice and the two boys arrived. On three sides of the rink a semicircle of rock-ledged hills sloped upward. Foliage on trees and shrubbery barely moved in the warm evening air. Lights from the Plaza, the St. Moritz, the Hampshire House on Central Park South formed a black and silver backdrop, while high overhead airplanes blinked their red and white lights and droned off to far places.

It was dusk and there were children everywhere, racing from parents or nursemaids, clamoring for popcorn and ice cream. Park policemen were constantly on the alert to keep them from darting into the gloom beyond the high wire fence that bounded the rink.

179

"Everybody-one-and-all!" The orchestra had begun playing and the announcer sang the calls for the square dance.

"Everybody! That's us!" Victor reached for Sharon's hand. "Come on, Dick! Janice!"

Other couples might wait until the rink was at least partially filled. Not Victor. With Dick and Janice trailing he led the way to the first circle forming in front of the orchestra.

"All-join-hands-and-now-around." It was a pleasant singsong.

Victor danced lightly and twirled Sharon easily. Dick, heavier and not so lithe, was less a part of the music and movement, but he danced well and Janice seemed to be having a good time.

"Square dancing in the heart of New York City!" She laughed when the set ended. "Let's get some popcorn. It's like a county fair. Kids, old folks, young folks!"

"After the next set," Victor said. "Come on, they're ready to start up again." He didn't want to miss a dance, and when he bowed left and right there was no doubt of his enjoyment. Sharon was having a good time, too; she had forgotten her disappointing interview with Mrs. Whiteman and the let-down feeling of the afternoon.

The evening was half over before popcorn was mentioned again, and the four started from the rink for the level above where soft drinks, ice cream and popcorn were sold. Half way up the steps Sharon stopped, scarcely able to realize that she was actually seeing Brad Johnson coming down.

"Dick! Look!" Then she began waving and Brad saw her. His smile of welcome was so genuine that she wanted to run to him.

"Sharon! I didn't know whether I'd find you or not. Dick! Gosh but it's good to see you."

He held out a hand to each. "I called your house all afternoon," Brad told Sharon after acknowledging the introductions to Janice and Victor. "Nobody answered. Finally I thought you might be up at the Y so I went over there, just to find you'd left only a few minutes before. I'd have caught up with you at dinner time only the program director roped me into something. Remind me to tell you about it. Finally I got your mother and she told me where you were."

He trooped along with them to the popcorn stand.

"Did you get our cards?" Dick asked. "Are you coming down for my graduation?"

"Yes, and to take you back up to the Cape with me," Brad promised. "This trip is an extra we can thank Debby for. She talked Dad into cruising down to New York instead of up to Portland so she and her mother can come back with us."

"Then this is the surprise!" Sharon knew it was. "She said I'd be surprised."

"You'll be surprised at the plans I've got for Dick, too," Brad said. "Wait until you see the fishing gear Dad's assembled. He's got the bluefish trained so they practically come when he whistles. But I don't suppose girls are interested in fishing. I'll tell you about it some other time. How's the music here?"

The musicians were tuning up again and over the loudspeaker came the chant: "Everybody-one-and-all."

Victor, who had not entered into the conversation with the two older boys, took Sharon's hand almost roughly and started down the steps ahead of the others.

"Do they allow cuts at a square dance?" she heard Brad

asking, but Victor ignored the question and hurried her even faster toward the rink.

"All-join-hands," he sang with the announcer and with a quick look at the assembling dancers, joined a circle which needed only one more couple for the set. Janice and Dick would not be with them this round and Brad, without a partner, was left behind.

Under the bright lights focused on the floor it was difficult to see people at the sidelines. Sharon looked back toward the stairway where she had last seen Brad, but she could not distinguish him in the crowd. Meanwhile Victor was dancing with even greater enthusiasm, humming the tunes and pressing her hand each time he took it. When the dance was over he started for seats at the far side of the rink.

"We won't find Dick and Janice over here," Sharon protested. It was Brad she was thinking of, and she felt certain Victor knew it.

"I don't want to find Dick and Janice," Victor said. "Or anyone else. You're my date, remember?"

"Of course, but we all came together."

"Must we stay together? The whole evening?"

Sharon tried not to show her displeasure, but there were so many things she wanted to talk over with Brad! She had scarcely seen him. What was he going to think if she didn't come back with Dick and Janice?

Victor found seats on an empty bench and lost no time in asking the question that was on his mind.

"Look, were you and this Brad going steady last year or anything like that?" It was his usual straight-to-the-point manner.

182

"No," Sharon admitted. "We had dated for more than a year, though."

"I suppose it's all right for him to follow you up here and want to cut in," Victor said. "Only . . . well, we were just getting started and I'd thought I'd like to keep on dating you."

Sharon looked at the toes of her nice pink shoes. These were the shoes, this was the aqua skirt and blouse she had worn the night she and Brad had been together for the last time before he left for the Cape. Was he waiting for her now on the opposite side of the rink? She didn't respond to Victor's implied question.

"Haven't you had a good time with me?" he persisted. "I've had such a swell time. I mean, I thought you were really swell. Didn't you have a good time?"

"Of course I've had a good time," she said, but she was thinking that he had ruined this date.

"You won't stop going with me? Just because he's back?"

Halfheartedly Sharon said no. Brad had dated Debby this summer. He'd never asked her to go steady.

"Then we'll go back and join the crowd after the next dance," Victor said. "He can even cut. I just wanted to get things straight."

After the dance, however, it was evident Brad had understood that Victor wanted no cuts. He had gone, but he had left a message; and while Janice was talking to Victor with more gusto than necessary, Dick passed it on.

"Our boy friend spoiled things for Brad tonight," Dick said, and he looked annoyed. "The program director at the Y was in a jam when he got there today. She has twenty-five kids lined up for a two-day trip to Bear Mountain and the fellow who was going to help ride herd on them came down with summer flu this morning. She talked Brad into taking his place, and he's leaving at daylight, so naturally he couldn't wait around. And he won't be back until late Sunday night."

"Oh, no!"

"And Monday they sail back to the Cape with Debby and her mother."

Sharon could have cried. The evening was really ruined now. The music and dancing were something to endure, and with a smile too if she didn't want to spoil things for the others. She was glad when it was over and she was on the way home, walking back through the park, past the still lagoon that mirrored the lights and the street scene above, past the rows of horse-drawn carriages lined up at the entrance to the park, all smelling of barns and old leather.

Was she going to see Brad again on this quick trip he had made to New York? How much had he and Dick settled about the outing they all had been dreaming about for months? She couldn't even ask about it now, since neither Janice nor Victor had been included. Brad hadn't met either of them until now.

She lay awake thinking about it that night, and it was on her mind Saturday until evening brought the excitement of a phone call from Janice's mother. Both Janice and Mother talked to her, and Janice laughed and cried at the same time when she was told she could stay in New York for one year, anyway.

Sharon wondered about that phone bill and was glad Aunt Agnes was paying it. Daddy, who was watching and listening, fumbled with his cold pipe and Sharon remembered that he had given up smoking weeks ago. She couldn't recall when he had been away for a job interview lately, and her happiness for Janice was mixed with concern for her father and her own disappointment at not seeing Brad.

On Sunday, Mother went with Sharon and Janice to Spelman Hall in the afternoon to look at the bedrooms and the big rooms where the girls worked and played and dated. In the evening Sharon scarcely budged from the living room. Her heart pounded every time the phone rang, but Brad didn't call. Then Monday morning he was there soon after she sat down to breakfast.

"I couldn't go without saying good-by," Sharon heard him explaining to Mother, who had answered the bell. "It was awfully late when I got the Y gang home last night, because the bus broke down. Now Dad wants to leave the house promptly at nine. You know where the boat basin is."

He walked into the living room, a bulky package under one arm, and he looked warm and uncomfortable. Sharon left her breakfast to go to him.

"I bought an album to take up to the Cape," he explained, and began unwrapping the package. "An oldie they were clearing out. It's the Paris Conservatory Orchestra and some Wagner. I bought one for you, too."

"Brad! We all will love it," Sharon said, and Mother thanked him too.

"Want to walk over to the park with me?" he asked. "There isn't much time and we still haven't made any very definite plans for the outing."

Of course she wanted to go.

The sun wasn't hot yet, sparrows chirped cheerfully, and

185

the few trees along Waverly Place nodded in the morning breeze while they walked along.

"How's the summer been going?" Brad asked. "I hear you've been doing something special at the Y."

It wasn't like Brad to be self-conscious, but the question sounded too formal and the comment too polite. Sharon glanced at his sun-browned arms, then up at his face. He wasn't looking at her, but toward the park ahead. She was sure she knew what was on his mind and feared he wouldn't ask the question that was troubling him. Somehow she must tell him about Victor, only how? He musn't think she was the one who had wanted to hurry back to the square dance; that she hadn't wanted him to cut in.

"Everything at the Y is just dandy, I guess," Sharon said. "It would be if Debby could come back and swim in the summer Aquacade. What are you planning? About coming down for Dick's graduation, I mean."

"Dick wants me to sail down again," Brad told her. "I guess I could talk Dad into it if everybody wants it that way."

"You could bring Debby down, couldn't you?" Sharon suggested. "I think she wants to come. Then we could all sail back up to the Cape, couldn't we?"

"That's what I've been planning. I hope everybody still wants to. Dick . . . you . . . Marie. I haven't even talked to Marie."

"She's counting on it," Sharon assured him. "We all are. We have been, all summer."

"Honestly?"

"Honestly, Brad!" She hoped he believed her. Hoped she was answering his unasked question. She started to say more but a cheerful voice called "Hi!" and Debby was running across the park toward them.

"Oh!" Sharon couldn't suppress a groan.

"She can always come at the wrong time, can't she?" Brad said, and his voice sounded more natural than before. "I'll try to get her down at the right time, for once. For your Aquacade, I mean."

She could only hope that he trusted her and understood; that he wasn't just being kind for old times' sake. Now Debby, outfitted in navy-blue slacks and shirt and bursting with cheerful chatter, was with them and the conversation had to change.

There was comfort, though, in the assurance that Brad was coming back for Dick's graduation and her Aquacade. They would have the week they had planned, too.

Sharon was able to take up her full schedule at the Y that week, since Frank Togliotti and his wife had flown home Sunday and she wasn't needed at the copper shop. Her enthusiasm for the typing class had flagged, however, after her interview with Mrs. Whiteman. She did manage to induce Lucille to come to the pool for two extra sessions.

Sharon had only one date with Victor before Dick's graduation, and it was just a couple of hours in the park listening to the band concert and eating ice cream. Somehow Victor had expected Dick to be there too, and Sharon felt he was disappointed in the evening. It hadn't been very exciting.

Graduation morning brought clear skies and a mellow breeze. It brought Victor again, dressed in a new suit and so excited about his first visit to Kings Point that he could talk of nothing else. Sharon's own excitement was clouded by concern. There had been no phone call from either Brad or Debby. She had jumped every time the phone rang the day before, and she was worried now. Had something gone wrong? Even Mother and Daddy were anxious. Then the call came through.

"Hi! Fleet's in."

"Brad! Am I glad to hear your voice!" She knew her relief was audible.

"There was considerable fog out here in the Sound last night," he told her. "Probably you landlubbers on Manhattan Island didn't know."

"No, I didn't know. There wasn't anything on the radio about it."

"It wasn't that bad, I guess. But the basin was so full of small craft it was like the subway, and Dad thought we should ride at anchor and not come in until morning."

He sounded like the old Brad.

"You could have swum," Sharon told him. "What about Debby?"

"I hate to tell you," he answered. "Her father brought some more V.I.P's up in the middle of last week, so at the last minute she had to cancel out. I must say this for her, Sharon. She was sick about it. How's the girl you've been coaching?"

"Terrible. But we all knew it from the start."

"Well, I'll see you in about an hour, won't I? You're coming in time for Baccalaureate?"

"Starting this minute. The whole family's here in the hall positively glaring at me for staying on the phone."

They weren't glaring, they were smiling. All but Victor.

188

Sharon's relief and her pleasure at hearing Brad's voice had been obvious to him.

The clattering, noisy and dirty ride on the Long Island Railway and the bus trip from Kings Point to the Academy grounds were memorable for one thing: Victor chose to ride with Jimmy. He didn't even exchange glances with her. It was his way of telling her he understood how she felt about Brad, she was sure; she was grateful, although there seemed to be no way of saying it.

Brad and his father were waiting with Dick at the entrance gates, and for the first time Sharon saw her cousin in his "whites." She had always thought he looked impressive in the blue uniform, even though his severe chin and heavy eyebrows kept him from being handsome. But in his whites! She didn't try to tell him how he looked, for Jimmy and Nancy and Cathy descended on him bodily. Daddy shook his hand proudly and the look on Victor's face was hero worship.

Sharon fell into step beside Brad when they went into the chapel for Baccalaureate. There were three separate services, Protestant, Catholic and Jewish, each conducted in large part by the Cadet-Midshipmen. The lighted candles at the altar, the flowers, the white-draped communion table and the services were deeply inspiring, and when Dick gave the Prayer of Installation, Sharon was glad no one could see her misty eyelashes.

Dick had arranged to have his guests eat luncheon in the mess hall, but he had to leave them to march in formation with the other cadets to the big building on the Quad. Brad and the Heaths had been at ceremonies at the Academy before and the crisp shouts of "Hop! Hip! Harip!" and the precision marching of the platoons were not new to them; but the spectacle held Victor spellbound.

"This is what Victor wants," Sharon said quietly to Brad while they strolled across the green lawn behind the marching Merchant Marines. "From the minute he saw Dick, this had been it. He's going to take the examinations next year and try out. I hope he makes it."

"It's an impressive sight, and an accomplishment," Brad admitted. "I thought about it myself after I'd met Dick."

Dick was waiting for them when they reached the mess hall, and with him was a beribboned officer whom he introduced as Captain Culver. The Captain shook hands with everyone, including the little girls, but it was evident that he wanted to talk to Mr. Heath.

"Dick tells me you're a scientist and that you're retiring," he said almost at once. "I'm going with the A-A Oil Company to their new development in Arabia and they're looking for trained men. I retire too, as of today."

"The A-A Oil Company," Daddy repeated. "You mean that there are positions open?"

"The personnel officer told me the last time I saw him that they were looking for men with skill and ability and brains and dependability," the Captain said proudly. "At sixty-five people aren't old any more, and some forward-looking industrialists realize that men our age have a lot to offer. More than younger men without our experience. I don't think the A-A have all positions filled yet, from the way the personnel officer talked."

Daddy took his handkerchief from his pocket and wiped his forehead, and Mother stepped quickly to his side.

190

"But I've got a family. A young family," Daddy said, and looked from Mother to Sharon and the youngsters.

"That's all to the good," Captain Culver said. "They want family people and they pay transportation. You'll find they have an excellent school, kindergarten through high school."

"Only through high school?" Mother asked. Her voice sounded weak, and the look she gave Daddy was pathetic. For a moment neither one spoke. Mother pushed at her hair nervously, and the quickened rise and fall of Daddy's shoulders betrayed his emotion.

"I'll take you to the personnel office tomorrow if you'd like," Captain Culver offered. "I'm going into the city on business anyway."

In the uncomfortable silence that followed Sharon thought she would choke. She knew why Daddy was hesitating even before he spoke.

"I guess I'll have to think about it," he said. "It would involve . . . well, the family. May I call you?"

She couldn't break into a conversation with dignified Captain Culver, but she wanted to rush to Daddy and tell him he musn't pass up this opportunity because of her. She would do anything they wanted her to do. Go to New York University . . . live where they wanted her to live. Maybe at Spelman Hall. This was the chance Daddy had been trying to find. Important work with a fine organization Even a chance to travel. She had wanted to travel. Now that she thought about it, Daddy had never been west of the Great Lakes in his life! Sharon felt she had to speak, but now everyone was crowding into the mess hall where underclassmen were passing big trays loaded with food and everyone was talking at once.

SHARON

That luncheon in the huge room filled with cadets and their families, the final orders to march resounding over the loud-speaker, the precision of that last parade to the semicircle in front of the main building, were all unreal to Sharon.

"Hip! Hop! Harip!" Even the voices of the cadets in charge of each platoon failed to hold her. She had thought she would sit next to her mother when the spectators took their places in chairs under the trees on either side of the graduating class, but Captain Culver had brought his wife to meet her parents. She could only guess at the questions being asked and answered before the overture by the Regi-- mental Band opened the exercises.

Sharon didn't try to listen to the speeches. Except when Dick marched to the platform to accept the American Bureau of Shipping Award, her mind wasn't on the ceremony. Those rows of young men in starched white uniforms and black-visored caps couldn't keep her mind off the crucial decision her father had to make and her realization that she was the determining factor.

"Is something the matter?" Brad finally whispered. "Is anything wrong? The Aquacade hasn't been called off, has it?"

The Aquacade. Sharon had even forgotten about that, and Brad would be there to see it. Brad and her entire family.

"Look! The boys are being sworn into the Naval Reserve," he told her. "When it's all over they're going to toss their old caps away. Everybody'll scramble for them. Dick's going to save his for Jimmy, but if Nancy and Cathy want one they'll have to jump."

He leaned over to whisper to the girls and after a moment

of wide-eyed surprise they slipped from their chairs to crowd at the edges of the semicircle.

"Want me to get one for you?" Brad asked.

Sharon was about to say no, but in a flash she saw a different picture and a different setting.

"Get two!" she told him. "I've got to have two!"

CHAPTER SIXTEEN

SUMMER AQUACADE

No ONE was in a hurry to leave the beautiful grounds, the cool breeze from the boat-speckled Sound, and the newly commissioned Ensigns except Sharon.

"Brad, I've got to get back," she told him when she had the two caps safely under her arm. "If you and the folks want to stay with Dick, it's all right. Victor's going to talk to Captain Culver or die trying. So if you don't mind I'm leaving."

"But everybody's going to stay around," Brad protested. "Nobody's rushing off. There's a snack bar over in the mess hall where we can get cold drinks. Later on there's to be a military wedding and Dick's one of the attendants. It'll be something to see, with swords shining and everything."

"There may be something to see at the Aquacade tomorrow night if I get back and start things moving," Sharon said. "There won't be if I don't. Believe me, we're pretty flat!"

195

"You mean . . ." He looked at the caps again. "You're going to try to copy the uniforms some way?"

Her idea for saving the Aquacade had carried over. There was admiration as well as surprise in Brad's voice.

"There's a sewing room at Spelman Hall and Janice will help," Sharon explained. "I'll call Miss Moore and some of the girls from here. But don't expect too much," she added.

"And I'd hoped we could have a date at last." He looked at her questioningly. "I'd thought we could help Dick celebrate tonight."

For a moment Sharon wavered. She didn't have to call Miss Moore and explain her idea. Perhaps it wouldn't work anyway. She wanted an evening with Brad very much. An evening uncomplicated by misunderstandings; a little time alone with him to explain what had happened up in Central Park, if an explanation was still necessary. Then she thought of the Aquacade. It was a weak imitation of last spring's gala event and that was all. This was the one way to make it different—a show in its own right.

"Couldn't we celebrate tomorrow night? After the Aquacade?" she asked. "You don't know how important it is because I haven't had time to tell you. Miss Moore's chance for a job at the Y depends on it. And more than that." She couldn't tell him how much depended on it now, and he didn't suspect.

"If it's that important to Miss Moore. . . ." Brad gave a sigh of resignation.

"It really is," Sharon insisted. "Right now I want to see Mother for a minute and then get started."

Brad looked at the group of people around her mother. Captain Culver was introducing other faculty members.

"I might make a flying tackle," he suggested. "Lend me those two caps and I'll wig wag a distress signal."

He waved a cap in the air, and Mother came in response to his nod in Sharon's direction. Thoughtfully he stepped aside while they talked.

"Mother, you're not going to let Daddy turn down that job, are you?" Sharon whispered. "Not on account of me."

Mother took Sharon's hand and held it firmly. "We'll talk about it tonight, dear," she said. "Now don't worry."

"Tonight I don't know when I'll get home," Sharon told her. "I'm going to call the girls in the Aquacade and see how many can help work out an idea I've just had for our bathing suits. They're so ordinary. Just plain white suits with those beat-up old foam rubber roses on the shoulders. I'm sure Janice can get the use of the sewing room at Spelman Hall, so I want to go right now and call Miss Moore and get started."

"Right now? On what?" Mother asked. Then she seemed to understand. "Oh, fixing the bathing suits! All right, run along, only don't go with that worried look on your face. You look positively distressed."

"I am," Sharon acknowledged. "About Daddy."

They stood under the trees beside the abandoned semicircle and Mother put her arm across Sharon's shoulders, unmindful of the chattering, moving crowd.

"You're a dear girl, Sharon," she said softly. "Now run along and work out your plans with Miss Moore. We'll talk things over later."

Sharon called Miss Moore and Liz while she was waiting for the train at Kings Point. They could be buying the black plastic and brass buttons, the needles and thread and elastic

197

that would be needed, while she was on the train coming home. Black visors to fit over white bathing caps, high black collars tight under the girls' chins, wide black belts and narrow connecting bands to set off brass buttons—in her mind's eye she could see how this would transform the bathing suits and give their Aquacade the snap and zing it lacked.

Daddy, however, more than the Aquacade, was on Sharon's mind during that ride back to the city. At Spelman Hall she would see the Director again, and she was determined to find out whether she could stay there next year if Daddy went abroad with the A-A Oil Company. She even thought she knew where the money could come from to pay her expenses. When she got home tonight she should have something worked out; something decided for herself so that Daddy could go with Captain Culver tomorrow and learn about the position.

It was after five o'clock when Sharon reached Spelman Hall. Miss Moore, four girls and Janice were waiting for her in the lobby, eager and excited over the sketchy news Miss Moore and Liz had been able to convey. Janice already had arranged the use of the sewing room.

"If we're going to pattern the costuming after the Merchant Marine graduation program and march into the room, I'll have to locate a good march record," Miss Moore said after Sharon had explained her idea fully. "About all we have is a collection of slow waltzes."

"We'll need a good march," Sharon agreed. "We've got to go in with a 'Hip! Hop! Harip!' and in miniature platoon formation."

"It's a terrific idea," Miss Moore agreed. "You girls go ahead and turn out the collars and belts and I'll hunt rec-

198

ords. I can't stay and help sew because I have an evening class again tonight."

Sharon hadn't seen the Director of Spelman Hall when the girls went to the sewing room, but when they stopped for a quick evening meal she looked into the office. All afternoon she had been thinking of what she would say. Now she felt nervous and timid. It hadn't been hard to ask questions for Janice. It was more difficult to interrupt the busy woman, bent over a pile of papers at her desk, and explain her own unexpected need for help.

Sharon cleared her throat and the Director looked up. "May I bother you? Just to ask a question?"

"Of course. You're Janice Ross's cousin, aren't you?"

"Yes, and now I've got a problem almost like Janice's," Sharon began. "If my father should go abroad in the fall and take the rest of the family with him, could I live here too? Would I be eligible? I wouldn't be on a scholarship like the girls from Liberia, but I'd be going to N.Y.U."

The Director smiled. "There isn't any rule against it," she said. "Have your mother talk to me about it."

Sharon knew she showed her relief. Tonight she would really have something helpful to say to her parents. She wouldn't be a headache and a worry for them as she had been all summer.

It was ten o'clock when the sewing group broke up. To-morrow morning a second shift of girls would come, and there would be plenty of time to finish the motifs for their bathing suits and get to the Y in time for a good practice session before the evening performance.

Mother and Daddy were in the living room when Sharon came in. The TV screen was gray and silent; they weren't watching their Thursday night shows. Sharon went to her father at once and sat on the arm of his chair.

"You're going to see the personnel man with Captain Culver tomorrow, aren't you?" she began at once. "I've got everything worked out for me, so you won't have to worry."

"You've got everything worked out?" Daddy asked, and Mother looked her surprise.

"I know you wanted me to go to New York University because you've always taught there," Sharon said, resting her cheek against her father's white hair. "So I'll go, and I can live at Spelman Hall. All Mother has to do is arrange it with the Director. If we sublet our apartment, wouldn't that pay my expenses?"

Daddy slipped his arm around Sharon's waist. "You're a real little worker-outer, aren't you?" He smiled and patted her knee with his free hand. "You're sort of important to your mother and me, you know. Quite as important as a job with the A-A Oil Company."

"But Daddy!"

"Look, honey, you've been protesting all summer that you didn't want to go to N.Y.U. If you don't want to go, and so violently, perhaps we shouldn't insist. Maybe you should stay out a year, or even two. You're not quite seventeen and most of the freshmen will be seventeen or eighteen."

"But what would I do, with you gone?"

"You'd come along with us, of course, if I get the job," Daddy explained. "Captain Culver's practically certain I'll qualify. The hitch is, we don't know what you'd do with yourself over there. I talked to the Captain again today and he wasn't certain about conditions. Tomorrow I'm going to see the personnel director and find out what there'd be for a girl your age to do. Whether there'd be any social life or interesting activities at the colony or settlement or whatever they call it. I'm afraid all the young people your age would be off in college someplace else."

Sharon hadn't thought of going to Arabia herself, and the unexpected proposal brought mental warning signals. Two years without seeing Brad or Marie or Debby. Two years out of school. Probably there wouldn't be anything interesting to do. It might be as boring as Martha's Vineyard had been for Debby, who'd had nothing to do all summer.

"I'm not too young to go to college," Sharon protested. "I'm almost seventeen. It was just that I didn't know what to take. I wouldn't have known any better out in Colorado, I know," she admitted. "Only there I'd have had so much fun living in dorms and skiing almost every day."

"There aren't any dormitories or beautiful campus grounds or any skiing at N.Y.U.," Daddy admitted. "All you could plan would be weekend snow trains now and then. We don't have to settle it tonight, though. Let's see what I can find out tomorrow."

"Sharon, you look so upset," Mother said. "Don't worry about it any more. You have a big day ahead of you tomorrow. Captain and Mrs. Culver are going to have dinner with us, and I've invited Dick and Brad. We're all going to your Aquacade and then dancing on the roof. Dick's going to call Janice the first thing in the morning. So now let's look at your clothes."

"You invited the Culvers? To the Aquacade?" Sharon asked her mother. "Didn't you know we're using the graduation at Kings Point as a motif? They'll think I shouldn't have done it. Maybe it won't be good!"

201

"Why, I think that's a lovely idea," Mother exclaimed. "Dick will love it. So will the Culvers. Now come along."

Sharon hoped that Dick and the Culvers would be pleased, but she couldn't help worrying. She slept restlessly that night and worked all the next day on the visors and belts and buttons for the bathing suits. They did add a great deal of snap and sparkle to the girls' appearance when they lined up at the pool to practice marching in before the performance began.

Sharon watched Miss Moore's expression anxiously and joined her at the record player where the instructor was putting the discs in proper order. "Suppose it doesn't go over?" she asked. "Suppose we just fall flat on our faces and all because of my big idea? I'd die if you lost the job because of this."

"You've a good, long life ahead of you if all it depends on our show tonight," Miss Moore replied. "I've just come from a session with the Director and I wanted to tell you before the performance begins. We're in, both of us. We may not have the best Aquacade the Y ever put on, but we got 'E' for effort anyway."

"You mean. . . ." Sharon couldn't believe it. "We're hired *before* the Aquacade? Even if the Director doesn't know whether it'll be any good or not?"

"She knows we've done the best we could with what we had. Look, Sharon, if you're going to be a recreation worker here at the Y, or with the Board of Education or anywhere else, you've got to realize that you can't always be the best. What we've accomplished with these girls this summer is what counts. Look at them, standing like soldiers—or Merchant Marines I should say—and without you! Look at Liz! Look at Lucille, stretching to her full five feet!"

Sharon looked, but she saw the girls through a haze as though they were a long way off. What had Miss Moore just said? "If you're going to be a recreation worker here at the Y. . . ." Of course that was it! Why had she floundered and made such a bad business of deciding what she was going to do?

"Miss Moore, do you honestly believe I could?" She knew her voice didn't sound natural. In her heart she was certain she could do it, but now she needed reassurance.

"Could what?"

"Be a recreation instructor some day? Like you."

"I supposed that was what you wanted to be," Miss Moore said and her brown eyes looked at Sharon questioningly. "Isn't it?"

"I guess so. I'm sure in fact. It's just that I hadn't dared to think of it."

The swimming instructor shook her head. "And with your talent for leadership and your ability in all sports! Honestly, Sharon there's something to that old song. . . ."

Miss Moore began humming and finally sang a few lines of a song about happiness "in your own back yard."

"Oh, Miss Moore! You'll never know what this night means to me!" Sharon exclaimed. "I'll really get in there and swim."

"That's one thing I'm positive of," Miss Moore assured her. "Yes, of that I'm certain."

Sharon could have sung for joy. Miss Moore's eyes were shining. Everything had turned out well for them both, and next year they would be working together every day. And tonight was going to be all right!

Every seat was filled and all standing room taken when the girls lined up in miniature platoon formation in the dressing room. Miss Moore stood beside them to give final instructions and encouragement before she went out to greet the guests and start the performance. Unexpectedly a side door opened and the Director of Central Y came in.

"You all look fine," she said. "I just stopped in to tell you how proud I am of you. I may not see everyone after the show. You've done a wonderful job. Miss Moore and Sharon, I'm really proud!"

She smiled encouragement at the rest of the group too and with a little gesture left them.

"She's proud of us, and we haven't done anything yet," Lucille gasped.

"Well, you're going to!" Sharon told her pupil. "This is *it*, girl!"

From the pool came the music of "The Stars and Stripes Forever." Sharon gave a last look at the two platoons and led the way.

"Hip! Hop! Harip!"

Around the pool to the starting place, Sharon and Liz with their Merchant Marine caps perched jauntily on their curls, the girls with little black visors over their white bathing caps. Then the record changed and the waltz strains cued them into the show. As a unit the girls dived into the pool and while they swam toward their places in the formation Sharon and Liz remained stationary, treading water, hands raised in military salute. When the circle formed they tossed the white caps to the gallery of visitors in true Merchant

Marine fashion and took their places—sure straight spokes to hold the wheel.

The applause was reassuring, the music sweet. From one routine to the next the summer group went through the ballet program. Even Sharon and Lucille were applauded for their over-arm close formation act. "E for effort," Sharon thought while she stayed with Lucille and kept the distance uniform.

It was difficult to get away after the show, so many girls crowded around the entrance to congratulate the swimmers. In the dressing room Sharon finally shook out her pretty blue dress with the pearls at the neckline which she had brought to the Y in her little overnight bag. Daddy and Mother, Captain and Mrs. Culver, Dick and Janice and Brad—best of all, Brad—would be waiting on the roof. The light wasn't too good in the dressing rooms and the mirrors were small, but she was finally dressed. She and Liz surveyed each other critically before leaving the floor.

She spied her friends and relatives as soon as she stepped out onto the lovely roof. They were at a table near the record player, and leaves of a big potted plant waving gently over them tickled Daddy's ear now and then. The air was cool, in contrast to the hot, moist atmosphere of the pool. Overhead an August moon hung low and the rosy reflection of Manhattan's neon world came up to meet it.

"Miss Kings Point!" Captain Culver said when she reached the table. "It's been decided I should be the first to congratulate you!"

Brad, tall and sun-tanned and smiling, was holding a chair for her. Dick, in his whites and with a new cap in one hand, extended the other in greeting. "I wish all the fellows could have seen you," he said, and he looked really proud.

"You think it was all right, then?" Sharon asked, taking her place at the table. "I was really nervous when Mother said she'd invited Captain and Mrs. Culver to the Aquacade."

"We all thought you were wonderful," Captain Culver assured her. "I expect some day I'll be seeing your name in headlines. 'Sharon Heath Conquers Red Sea!'" He laughed heartily.

"Not the Red Sea," Sharon laughed back. "I'll try swimming around Manhattan Island first. I . . . well, I guess I can tell it now. I've been given the job of assistant swimming instructor here at the Y next year. Miss Moore's going to be instructor and I'm to help her after school and nights and Saturdays. We just learned the news before the show."

"You've been offered a job?" Daddy sounded incredulous.

"At the Y?" Plainly Brad was surprised too, but there was approval in his smile and voice.

Then they all were asking questions at once.

"The Director said we deserved it," Sharon explained. "She told Miss Moore this afternoon, before we'd put on the Aquacade, and Miss Moore told me just before the show. It was thrilling!"

She looked at her father and smiled confidently. "You know what I'm going to do, Daddy? I should have known it all along. I'm going to be a recreation worker like Miss Moore. She took all her college work here at Columbia, and she didn't have a part-time job at first the way I'll have, either. When I finish college I'm almost sure of a job, don't you think?"

"You've scarcely given me time to think," Daddy said.

"My snap judgment would be yes, it should work out that way. Everything should work out all right for all of us."

Captain Culver nodded knowingly. "I'm sure it will," he said.

"I'd say Sharon's done all right," Brad observed, and he looked pleased. "Now tomorrow morning we can start for Cape Cod with everything settled—even the future—and not a worry in the world."

"I thought this week would never come," Sharon said and sighed with relief. "Now tomorrow it starts."

The girls at the record player were fumbling with discs and Brad moved his chair back to watch them. "I wish they'd get this dance going," he said quietly. "I'll tell you more about what I think when they do."

"Let's help them," Sharon suggested. She knew the record she wanted to have played first, and she walked to the table and began looking through the labels. Brad followed her.

"Here's an oldie and silly under the circumstances, I guess." She handed the girl the number that had been at the top of Brad's own hit parade.

"This is where I've been wishing you were for weeks," Brad whispered when he took her into his arms. With the music he sang the words softly—"Wish you were here."

HARRIETT H. CARR

HARRIETT CARR knows her Greenwich Village because she lived there for years. She moved to New York from Michigan, where she worked on a large daily paper after studying at the Michigan State Normal College and the University of Michigan. There she says she got "All A's in literature, writing, journalism and radio; all flunks in science and math!"

Since then she has continued to get A's in writing and journalism, figuratively speaking, for she has a responsible magazine job and has published five books since she landed in the big city.

These are *Gravel Gold* and *Borghild of Brooklyn* (Junior Literary Guild) Ariel Books; and *Where the Turnpike Starts, Against the Wind,* and *Miami Towers,* Macmillan Company.

841